"Tell me your name," she said against his mouth.

"Rudy," he said, kissing her again.

"Please," she breathed. "I need…"

He kissed her hard and deep. Sabine thought her eyes would roll backward from the sensations firing through her.

"Tell me your real name," she barely managed to say. "Tell me," she urged.

He looked down at her. A long moment passed.

"Cullen."

"Cullen." She looked into his eyes and gave him another kiss. "Cullen. Cullen. Cullen." She met his mouth again. When she withdrew, she opened her eyes and found his.

"Make love to me, Cullen."

Dear Reader,

Let's extend our summer lovin' with this month's Silhouette Romantic Suspense offerings. Reader-favorite Kathleen Creighton will enthrall you with *Daredevil's Run* (#1523), the latest in her miniseries THE TAKEN. Here, an embittered man reunites with his long-lost love as they go on a death-defying adventure in the wilderness. You'll feel the heat from Cindy Dees's *Killer Affair* (#1524), the third book in SEDUCTION SUMMER. In this series, a serial killer murders amorous couples on the beach, and no lover is safe. Don't miss the exciting conclusion to this sizzling roller-coaster ride!

When a handsome hero receives a mysterious postcard, he joins forces to find its sender with the woman who secretly loves him. Can they overcome a shared tragedy and face the future together? Find out in Justine Davis's emotional tale *Her Best Friend's Husband* (#1525), which is part of her popular REDSTONE, INCORPORATED miniseries. Finally, let's give a big welcome to Jennifer Morey, who debuts in the line with *The Secret Soldier* (#1526), and begins her miniseries ALL McQUEEN'S MEN. In this action-packed story, a dangerous—and ultrasexy—military man must rescue a kidnapped scientist. As they risk life and limb, they discover an unforgettable chemistry.

This month, you'll find love against the odds and adventures lurking around every corner. Enjoy these gems from Silhouette Romantic Suspense!

Sincerely,

Patience Smith
Senior Editor

The
SECRET SOLDIER
Jennifer Morey

Barbara Lea Kozak

Silhouette®
Romantic
SUSPENSE

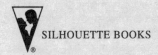

SILHOUETTE BOOKS

ISBN-13: 978-0-373-27596-0
ISBN-10:   0-373-27596-X

THE SECRET SOLDIER

Visit Silhouette Books at www.eHarlequin.com

Printed in U.S.A.

Books by Jennifer Morey

Silhouette Romantic Suspense

The Secret Soldier #1526

JENNIFER MOREY

has been creating stories since she fell in love with *The Black Stallion* by Walter Farley. She has a B.S. in geology from Colorado State University and is now program specialist for the spacecraft systems segment of a satellite imagery and information company. She holds a Secret-level security clearance. Jennie has received several awards for her writing, one of which led to the publication of her debut novel, *The Secret Soldier*. She lives in Loveland, Colorado, with her yellow Lab and golden retriever.

Special thanks go to Dave Baker for letting me have my way in the opening scenes of this story. Dave, those hours in front of your white board were sure entertaining! You have an amazing brain and your knowledge of the military was invaluable to me. Any mistakes are my own.

To everyone who supported me on my long journey to publication, your positive influence kept me going at my lowest moments. Everyone at DigitalGlobe—there are too many to name you all. You know who you are.
Gary Geissinger, don't worry, you won't end up in my novel. Neal Anderson and Walter Scott, any other bosses would have fired me for taking so much time off to write! Natalie Ottobrino and Margie Lawson, your strength resonates with me. To my entire family, who put up with my many absences so I could write. Dan, even though we aren't together anymore, you were an integral part of my success and will always be my friend. Jackie, you are my favorite twin—despite your poor taste in fiction. To Sandra Kerns and Annette Elton, for helping me make sure my characters didn't do anything too stupid. And to every other critique partner I have learned from along the way.

But the highest acknowledgment goes to my mother, Joan Morey, whose passing inspired me to follow my heart.

Chapter 1

"One more week in this hellhole."

Kneeling on the ground, Sabine O'Clery finished winding a water-level indicator reel from inside a borehole before looking up at her unhappy field partner. Samuel Barry scowled across the grayish-brown landscape of Afghanistan's Panjshir Valley. Sabine followed his gaze, a dry, hot breeze rustling the loose strands of hair that had escaped her ponytail. High, desolate mountains surrounded them under a clear blue sky, and yellow patches of grass covered the ground where they worked. She found immense satisfaction putting her hydrogeology degree to good use in places like this, but she couldn't argue with Samuel's sentiment.

"It's pretty here," she quipped.

Samuel grunted in disgust. "Yeah, if you like dirt and no amenities."

"Everyone needs clean drinking water," she said. She'd grown attached to some of the villagers, too.

Samuel grumbled as he put a portable reader on the ground next to the borehole. He was a big man who always talked about his wife.

"I can't wait to taste Lisandra's homemade orange juice," he said, as if on cue.

Sabine smiled. Would she ever find a man who made her feel like talking sweet nonsense about him? Ha! She wasn't going to hold her breath.

"She makes a killer crème brûlée, too."

"And her cheese soufflés?" she teased.

Samuel laughed. "My mouth is watering already." He looked at her. "Sorry. I just miss her."

"Really? I couldn't tell."

"Just wait 'til you get married. Then you'll know what it's like."

Marriage seemed so foreign to her. "Not everyone falls madly in love and lives happily ever after."

"Maybe not out here." He gestured to the dry landscape. The pages of the field book he held flapped with the movement, his thumb keeping the ones against the cover flat.

Maybe not ever. She didn't want to end up like her mother, loving a man who came around only when it suited him, always leaving for his next thrill. Nothing irritated her more than being treated like a thrill.

"You have to stop comparing every man to your dad," Samuel said.

She set the indicator reel aside and reached for the borehole reader, wishing she'd never mentioned her father to him. "I don't." Not *every* man.

He sent her an unconvinced frown from above the field book but didn't argue.

"I haven't seen him since he showed up at my college graduation and ruined what should have been my best accomplishment. Why would I compare anyone to him?"

Samuel raised a brow, telling her without words that the emotional response had just answered her own question.

Okay, so he was right. Her father epitomized the kind of man she never wanted to marry. She remembered the way she had felt when he'd shown up at her graduation. Unchecked hope that he'd come for the right reason flashed before a too-familiar self-doubt. Did he know about that B she got her freshman year? Never mind the honors. Maybe hydrogeology wasn't scientifically challenging enough. If she'd become the first female president of the United States, her father probably still wouldn't have been impressed.

So why waste any energy thinking of him at all? It wasn't supposed to bother her anymore. She'd overcome her insecurities and childish hopes the moment she left him standing in that college auditorium.

Connecting the reader to the piezometer inside the borehole harder than necessary, Sabine waited for the measurement to appear on the display. Samuel wrote the number down in his field book, eyeing her dubiously.

She'd never seen what real happiness looked like until she met her field partner. Maybe that's what had her thinking about her father so much lately. Happiness was not a word she'd learned from his example.

She straightened from the borehole. They were finished for the day.

"Let's go see if our supply helicopter brought us some cold beer." Samuel closed his field book.

"If Aden came with it, there'll be beer." As CEO of Envirotech and the one who had contracted them to do the groundwater analysis, Aden Archer always made room in the supply helicopter for good beer.

"He sure does come here a lot. Have you noticed that?"

"He doesn't come here that much."

"He doesn't need to be here at all."

She didn't think it was that unusual. "I saw him meet with one of the locals once. Maybe it's business related."

Samuel's brow creased as he looked at her. "Who'd he meet?"

She shrugged. "I didn't recognize him. All I saw was the back of his head."

It took him a moment to respond. "Don't you think that's a little weird? Why would he need to meet with any of the locals?"

"Who knows." Was Samuel as concerned as he seemed? Why? "He isn't hurting anyone."

Samuel looked at her a moment longer before he smiled, convincing her she'd misread him. "Especially if he brings beer. Come on, let's go." He started to walk toward the Jeep.

Sabine followed. She didn't feel like drinking beer. What she'd really like was a long, hot bath. With bubbles. And a good fantasy of a man who cherished her more than anything else in his life.

She breathed a laugh. Samuel's daydreaming was starting to rub off on her, apparently.

The sound of a vehicle made her stop and turn with a rush of alertness. No one ever came to see them out here. A pickup truck with the cab cut off bounced along the terrain. Several dark-skinned men were inside. Her heart slammed into a wild beat. They all held automatic weapons.

Samuel swore and dropped his field book before taking her hand to pull her ahead of him. She tripped as she started to run, her hand slipping free of his. Get to the Jeep. That was her only thought as she pumped her legs as hard as she could. But she could already see that the Jeep was too far away.

They weren't going to make it.

Oh God, please no.

She heard Samuel's heavy footfalls behind her. Hard breathing. More swearing.

"Run faster!" he yelled.

She didn't have to be told. If they were caught…

She couldn't think it.

Gunfire exploded. Sabine screamed and scrambled to dodge the spitting dirt where bullets struck the ground. The truck skidded to a halt between them and the Jeep. More bullets sprayed at their feet, forcing them to stop running.

Several men jumped off the open truck, shouting in Farsi, "Don't move! Don't move!"

Samuel grabbed Sabine's arm and pulled her behind him. She wanted to keep running. Instinct urged her to get away. But they'd shoot her if she tried. Shaking, she peered around Samuel's big arm and watched in horror as rebels surrounded them.

After a stuffy flight from Washington, D.C., Cullen McQueen left Miami's sweltering heat and entered Executive Indemnity Corporation. A security guard behind a reception desk looked up and smiled.

"I'm here to see Noah Page," Cullen said. "He's expecting me."

"Your name?"

"Henrietta," Cullen answered.

The man nodded his understanding and stood. He led Cullen to a locked door and let him through. Cullen entered a sprawling office area surrounded by closed doors. He spotted a woman standing near one of them.

She smiled. "You can go right in, Mr.…."

"Thanks." He smiled back at her and went into the conference room. Only one person knew his name here, and he was going to keep it that way.

Noah Page stood with his arms behind his back, staring out a panel of tinted windows on the far side of the room. He turned as Cullen shut the door. His face was lined and pale. Dark circles matched the grave worry in his blue eyes and his gray hair looked as if he'd run his fingers through it several times.

Cullen walked the length of the long conference room table and stopped before Noah, shaking his hand.

"Thank you for coming on such short notice," Noah said.

"You said it was urgent. Something about your daughter?"

Noah swallowed, a scared reflex. The notion of a man like Noah Page being scared piqued Cullen's curiosity. And a heap of foreboding.

"She's been kidnapped."

Cullen went still. "Do you know where she is?"

"Yes… Afghanistan. The Panjshir Valley."

That was in the mountains. The Hindu Kush. There weren't many worse places Noah's daughter could have been captured. "What's she doing there?"

"She's a contractor for Envirotech. She and another contractor were assessing groundwater conditions near one of the villages in the valley when they were abducted. I need you to get her out of there, Cullen. You're the only one I know who can do it."

Cullen laughed without humor. "You must have me confused with God."

"No." Noah sounded certain. "You know the terrain. You've done this kind of mission before. You do it all the time."

Not suicide missions, Cullen thought. He curbed his instinct to flat-out refuse Noah. "I know you're worried about your daughter, but you have to realize how difficult it will be to get her out of there. Not only is Afghanistan unstable, it's landlocked. You'd have to cross Indian and Pakistani ground defenses to get there." That didn't even begin to address U.S. forces inside the border.

"I've already met with the Minister of the Interior in Pakistan. He's agreed to clear you a flight plan into Afghanistan. There are regularly scheduled flights we can use as cover."

Cullen just stared at him.

"I've also procured two armed Mi-8 transport helicopters capable of flying high altitudes, one for backup and to carry extra fuel," Noah continued. "You'll have a DeHavilland Twin Otter equipped with a special jamming pod. It's been modified to fly long distances, too. I spared no expense on the equipment."

Rising tension tightened Cullen's jaw. He could not agree to this. But it was Noah asking.

"She's all I have left," Noah said in the silence, a pleading sound that didn't match the man. "I wouldn't ask if I had any other option." He leaned over the conference room table and pushed a newspaper toward Cullen.

Slowly, Cullen lowered his gaze. The page covering the kidnapping of two American contractors was exposed. Cullen had read about the kidnapping and seen it all over the news, but he'd never connected the name Sabina O'Clery with Noah Page. The media had stirred huge public interest in the female contractor who'd been taken by terrorists along with her partner, Samuel Barry.

He looked at the photo of Sabine. She smiled wide and bright, green eyes dancing with life, red hair long and thick. She was a beautiful woman. He'd thought so the first time he'd seen the photo. He'd also thought with regret that she would probably be killed before anyone could do anything.

Cullen raised only his eyes to look at Noah. Why did it have to be Afghanistan?

"You're my only hope of seeing my daughter alive again," Noah said quietly, urgently. "I've made mistakes in my life, but this one will kill me if she dies over there. Before I have a chance to make things right with her."

Cullen wanted to groan out loud. How could he say no? To Noah. Any other man, he'd already have been walking out the door. But Noah...

He couldn't say no. He had to do it. He owed Noah too much.

"It's going to take time to plan," he heard himself say.

Noah closed his eyes, a sign that he recognized Cullen's indirect agreement. "How much time?"

"A week. Maybe less. I have to be careful." And wasn't that just the understatement of the year.

Noah nodded. "I know you'll do the best you can."

Even his best might not keep him alive, but he held that thought to himself. "What kind of intelligence do you have?" Cullen looked down at the table and saw a map and several satellite images.

"Before we talk strategy, there's something you need to understand about my daughter."

Cullen looked back at Noah and waited. What could possibly matter when her life was on the line?

"She despises me."

Cullen couldn't stop his brow from rising.

"She has for years," Noah continued. "Ever since she was old enough to think on her own."

"I'm sure she'll change her mind once she sets foot on American soil again, compliments of you."

Noah shook his head. "You don't understand. You can't tell her I sent you."

"What do you want me to—"

"If you tell her I sent you, she'll find her own way home as soon as you get her out of Afghanistan. I know her. She won't stay with you."

"What am I supposed to say to her? I can't tell her who I am, either." What he did for his government privately had to stay private. No official could admit to asking him to do the things he did in the name of the United States. He couldn't risk telling Noah's daughter anything, especially knowing she was estranged from her father. And then there was the media hype to consider.

"Tell her whatever you want," Noah said. "Hell, lie to her if you have to. Just get her to me. I'll explain everything to her then."

* * *

What was that? Had she imagined the sound? Sabine felt every heartbeat in her chest as she lifted her head from where her aching body lay curled on a hard cement floor. She tried to see across the small cell that had been her prison for more than two weeks. Blackness stared back at her. None of this was real, was it? So much horror couldn't be real.

The rapid staccato of a man shouting something in Farsi convinced her well enough that she wasn't dreaming. She pushed herself to a sitting position, her body trembling from lack of water and food and, more than anything, from fear, as she scooted to the wall behind her, away from the door. Strands of her long, dirty red hair hung in front of her face, shivering with the tremors that rippled through her.

The door creaked open and one of her captors stepped in, holding a paraffin lamp. Beady eyes leered at her above an unkempt, hairy face. The others called him Asad. He wasn't their leader, but he frightened her nearly as much.

Glancing behind him, he closed the door. Sabine pressed her back harder against the cement wall as he approached, wishing it would miraculously give way and provide an escape.

Asad crouched close to her and put the lamp down beside him. He reached to touch her hair. Many of the other men seemed taken with the color, too.

Had Asad managed to slip away tonight? His presence this late and the look in his dark eyes said as much. Where was Isma'il? Would he stop him as he had all the other times?

She pulled away from Asad's hand and scrambled along the wall until the corner stopped her.

Anger brought Asad's brow crowding together. "Move when you are told," he said in Farsi.

If she lived, Sabine promised herself she'd never speak the language again and forget she'd ever studied it in college.

Standing, Asad stepped toward her and crouched in front of her again. She turned her face toward the wall and squeezed her eyes shut as he took strands of her hair between his fingers. "I will know this fire," he murmured, making her stomach churn.

"I'd rather die," she whispered in perfect Farsi, a soft hiss of defiance that belied her weakened state.

He let go of her hair but pulled back his hand for momentum and swung down to strike her face. Sabine grunted with the force of the blow, her head hitting the wall and one hand slapping the floor to stop her fall. She spit blood.

Voices outside the door of her cell made Asad pivot in his crouched position. He watched the door. When it began to open, he straightened.

"Isma'il is asking for you," a man said through the shadows.

Asad muttered an expletive and turned to look down at Sabine. Whatever he'd come to do to her tonight had once again been thwarted. She watched his anger flare with the snarl of his mouth. "The day will come when Isma'il will not interfere," he said. "And then you will die just as your friend did." With that, he picked up the lamp and turned to leave.

A shaky breath of relief whooshed out of her. Why was Isma'il protecting her? Terrorists would have no regard for a female captive. But who were they, if not terrorists? Were they holding her for ransom? Had they contacted Aden? Was he trying to save his contractors? Perhaps he'd lost some ground and that was why Samuel had been killed. She had no way of knowing. Her captors never spoke of their purpose in front of her and Samuel.

Samuel. She couldn't grasp that he was dead. They'd tortured and killed him. And they'd do the same to her. It was only a question of when.

Her soft, defeated sobs resonated against the cement walls that trapped her in this hellish place. She didn't want to die like this. Curling her body on the cement again, she stared through the darkness, trying to think of something to console her spirit. Fuel her strength.

Thoughts of her mother were too painful. She couldn't reconcile the difference between this place and the quiet innocence of Roaring Creek, Colorado, where her mother had raised her. Mae O'Clery was as much a best friend as she was a mother. When Mae told her this contracting job wasn't her calling, that she was doing it only to catch her father's attention, she should have listened. That arrowing insight had annoyed her at the time. But now, after being kidnapped and facing a horrific death, she could see the truth.

Unrelenting. That's how she had been when she'd gone after her college degree, and that's how she was in pursuing her career. Nothing had stopped her from proving to the world that she was…what? Tough? Smart? That she was worthy of envy and respect? She didn't like to admit that her relationship with her father had driven her to this moment, but it had. Amazing how his occasional visits to her mother had bled over into every aspect of her life. She wasn't good enough just the way she was. She had to try harder. Always harder.

A sound outside the door made her stiffen, lift her head. Had Isma'il sent for her? Was tonight her time to die?

Her heart beat so fast it made her sick. A hissing noise followed by a sort of zap sent a burst of light through spaces in the door frame.

Surely her mind was playing tricks on her. Wouldn't her captors use a key? Why was someone using strange explosives on the door?

The door swung open. A tall figure appeared. Silhouetted by meager light in the doorway, the man stood with an automatic weapon ready to fire. The folds of his black clothes and body armor encased a powerful body that was at least twice the size of any of her captors'. He turned first to his left, then scanned the room until he saw her.

Her heart felt like it skipped several beats as she watched him turn to look over his shoulder and make quick, firm gestures with his hand, holding the automatic rifle with the other. Slinging a strap over his shoulder, he hung the rifle against his back and approached.

Sabine wavered between elation and fear. Dare she hope this man had come to free her?

The tall man knelt in front of her, a small scope attached to his helmet and positioned in front of one eye. She guessed it was some sort of night-vision device. He was laden with other gear, too. A pistol strapped to his waist. Straps around his thighs from his parachute. A wide, dark backpack and several bulky pockets gave the appearance of size. Not that he was small; he had to be at least six-five and was no rail of a man.

"Are you injured?" he asked, putting his hand on her shoulder.

She jerked away from his touch, so conditioned to fear that the reaction was automatic.

He pulled his hand up as though in surrender. "I'm from the United States. I'm going to get you out of here. Do you understand?"

English. Her brain swirled in reverse and forward and sideways. He spoke *English*. And not just any English. He had a distinctive Western swagger to his vowels, strong and confident, marking him a wholly, one-hundred-percent, proud-to-be-American man. She couldn't let herself believe it, yet she felt her head nod twice.

"Where is Samuel Barry?" he asked.

Reminded of Samuel's death, the swell of tears renewed in her throat. "I…I'm the only one left."

The tall man's only reaction was the grim set of his mouth as he flipped another device down from his helmet.

"I've got the package. There's only one," he said into the small radio that arched in front of his mouth. "Have you found anything?"

"We're searching, sir," a voice came across the radio, barely audible. "So far nothing's turned up."

"Set the explosives and keep looking. Kill anything that moves."

"Roger that."

The tall man flipped the radio back against his helmet. There was nothing emotional about him. He was focused on his purpose, and right now that seemed to be getting her out of there.

"Can you stand?" he asked.

She didn't know and he didn't wait for an answer. He helped her to her feet with one arm around her back. She welcomed his strength as he supported her to the door. There, he leaned her against the wall beside the opening. She heard sounds outside. Something moving in the street.

Had her rescue been discovered?

"Don't move," the tall man said, his eye gleaming through the shadows, the other concealed behind the night-vision device.

Sabine didn't think she could move if she tried, she was so weak. Her legs were already trembling with the effort to keep her upright.

Pulling his weapon from his shoulder, the tall man peered outside. He had wide cheekbones and a prominent brow that gave his intense eyes a fearsome set. She didn't know how much time passed before she heard the sound of footfalls. The tall man made hand gestures through the open door, then shrugged his weapon back over his shoulder. He bent to lift Sabine, his arms under and behind her.

She looked over his shoulder as he carried her through the door of the small, six-by-six concrete cell that had been her home for so long. A crippling wave of remorse consumed her.

She was leaving without Samuel. *His wife.* What would it do to her when she found out about her husband? Sabine squeezed her eyes shut to a grief that would stay with her always.

Outside the door the tall man joined two other men dressed like him. Aiming their weapons, the other men flanked the tall man as he carried her into the street. Two bodies were sprawled on the ground near the door of the concrete cell. She hoped one of them was Asad.

"Find anything?" the tall man asked.

"Negative."

"Detonate when we reach the Mi-8."

"With pleasure, sir."

The two other men swung their weapons on either side of the tall man as they moved across the street.

Shouts erupted behind them. The tall man ran faster while his partners turned and jogged backward, aiming their weapons and firing. Over the tall man's shoulder, she saw three figures drop in the distance, lifeless shadows in the night.

The tall man slowed his pace as he carried her through an alley. One of his partners moved ahead and the other fell back. They emerged onto another street. Bombed-out buildings and burned shells of vehicles echoed a violent tale of the past.

The woof, woof of a helicopter sounded in the distance. The bombed-out buildings thinned as they came to the outskirts of the deserted village where her captors had taken her and Samuel. Sabine could make out the dark shape of a helicopter just ahead of them.

One of the tall man's partners jumped into the helicopter. The tall man handed her over to him. He swooped her through a narrow door and inside the pod, and she found herself lowered onto a toboggan-like stretcher. The interior of the helicopter had no seats, but the exposed metal walls contained small round windows. It was dim inside.

Sabine kept her gaze fixed on the tall man. He stood to one side of the opening as the helicopter lifted into the air. One of his partners knelt beside him. Both aimed their guns at the ground. The man kneeling depressed a remote of some sort. What she could see of the night sky lit up, and the sound of a giant explosion followed. Something pricked her arm.

Sabine looked up at the man kneeling beside her. In the light of the fire, she could see his brown hair and blue eyes. He smiled at her while he inserted the IV.

"You're goin' to be okay now," he said with a rich Southern drawl.

God bless America, she thought.

Gunshots made her grip the sides of the stretcher. Bullets sprayed the helicopter, and it dipped. It felt like something vital had been hit. Some of her captors must have survived and discovered her escape.

The man who'd inserted her IV scrambled to the cockpit.

"We're in big trouble if this thing goes down!" the pilot shouted, barely audible over the noise of the rotor.

The helicopter swayed and rattled amidst rounds of machine-gun fire.

"I can't go back there." Sabine struggled to raise her body. She crawled on her hands and knees toward the open door of the helicopter, heedless of the IV that ripped free of her arm and the sting of her raw shins, where her captors had beaten her the most. She searched for a weapon and spotted the pistol in the tall man's holster. When she reached for it, he put his hand around her wrist and stopped her.

"They're out of range now," he told her, one knee on the floor. "And you're not going back there."

Realizing the sound of gunfire had ceased, Sabine sagged at his words, falling flat onto her stomach with her forehead to the metal floor of the helicopter. Sobs came unbidden. They shook her shoulders and made her gasp for air. Relief. Gratitude. A cacophony of emotion too strong to subdue.

The tall man put his automatic rifle aside. She heard it settle on the floor of the helicopter. Sitting down, he reached for her. She let him pull her onto his lap, the promise of kindness from another human being too great to resist. Air from the opening at her back blew through her hair. She dug her fingers into the sturdy material of the tall man's body armor, resting her head on his shoulder until her tears quieted.

With a shuddering breath, Sabine inhaled the oily smell of the helicopter, the smell of freedom. Comfort she hadn't felt in weeks washed through her deprived soul. She wanted to stay close to the man who held her so warmly, his hand slowly moving over her back. He cradled her thighs with one arm, his hand pressed over her hip to hold her on his lap.

Sabine leaned back. Gray eyes fringed by thick, dark lashes looked down at her beneath the edge of his black helmet. He'd moved the night-vision device out of the way. There was sympathy in his eyes but something else, a hovering alertness, a readiness for combat. Her awareness of him grew. Those gray eyes.

His black hair sprouted from beneath the helmet, and she noticed for the first time that it hung low on the back of his neck. A few strands tickled the top of her hand. Lines bracketed each side of his mouth, his lips soft and full but unmoving. His jaw was broad and strong and covered with stubble.

"What's your name?" she asked, wanting to think of him as something other than a tall man.

"You can call me Rudy," he answered after a slight hesitation.

The sound of more gunfire made Sabine look through the door into the night sky. She spotted another helicopter firing at them. Rudy tossed her off his lap at the same instant bullets struck metal. She landed on her rear in a pile of gear and packs in the back of the helicopter. Rudy grabbed his weapon and fired alongside one of his teammates.

"What the—" the man beside Rudy was cut short when a bullet put a hole in his forehead. He fell forward, out of the helicopter. It happened quickly, but Sabine knew violence like this all too well. The helpless sorrow swimming through her was familiar, something that had clung to her through her captivity.

Rudy fired his weapon again. Explosions of answering gunfire throttled along with the roar of rotor and blades. Bullets struck the helicopter's interior, plugging holes in the stretcher where Sabine had lain. She covered her head and buried herself among the gear as much as she could, moaning. Exhaustion did nothing to dull the sickening fear that had been her constant companion for so long.

Then the flurry of gunfire died. Sabine lifted her head. Rudy crouched, ready for battle.

"Who the hell was that?" the Southern man asked from his seat in the cockpit.

The helicopter sputtered and lost elevation with a severe plunge. The pilot cursed.

"What's our position?" Rudy demanded.

The pilot shouted back coordinates.

"Can you make it to the airstrip?"

"Maybe." The helicopter sputtered more. The pilot shook his head. "I don't know."

Sabine looked at Rudy. He glanced her way, and she saw his confusion. He hadn't expected to be attacked after lifting off the ground. The gunfire from the ground had been from what was left of her captors, but who had fired at them from the other helicopter?

"We're going down, we're going down!" the pilot yelled.

"No," Sabine breathed.

Rudy pushed away from the opening. Tossing his weapon aside, he landed on Sabine with the agility of a cat as the helicopter began to smoke and spin.

Chapter 2

Sabine screamed as the helicopter careened toward the ground. She could feel the pilot trying to keep the machine airborne. The roar was deafening. Debris flew through the pod. If it weren't for Rudy holding her, she'd have gone flying, too. But even he couldn't withstand the force of the crash. When they hit, she felt the jarring impact and knew her body had smashed against something hard, but she blacked out an instant later.

She regained consciousness to the smell of smoke and stillness. Flickers of fire alarmed her. She didn't know how long she'd been out. She didn't think it was longer than seconds or minutes.

Someone stirred beside her. She looked to see Rudy climb to his feet. He scanned the rest of the helicopter. The cockpit was barely visible through darkness and smoke and the tangle of metal.

"Comet!" Rudy shouted. "Blitz!"

There was no answer.

Sabine ignored the searing pain that sliced through her already bruised body and rose to her hands and knees. Rudy hefted a rucksack over his shoulder and stepped over scattered debris on his way to her. She grabbed his arm and used it as a tether to pull herself up. Instead of helping her walk out of the helicopter, Rudy bent and draped her over his big shoulder like a sack of dog food. She withheld groans of agony the pressure against her ribs caused.

Rudy hurried out of the helicopter. When he was far enough away, he lowered her to the ground. She sat on her rear—more like collapsed—and watched him drop the rucksack and jog back toward the helicopter for the other two.

An explosion flipped him onto his back. Sabine cringed and twisted away from the violent flames and rumbling blast. She rolled onto her side and covered her head as debris dropped from the air. A brief moment later, she pushed herself up by one hand and gaped at the inferno. Were the men still in there? They were, but she couldn't bring herself to face it. She crawled toward the helicopter, half sobbing, too numb to process everything all at once. She only knew she couldn't leave the men in that helicopter after they just saved her life.

She got as far as Rudy, who swung his arm out like an iron bar and stopped her. His face was stark with shock and maybe a few signs of grief. She didn't know him enough to read his emotions, but losing what must be his team had to be shattering.

Slowly, he turned his head. His eyes went from disbelieving to expressionless to angry before he eventually covered that, too. Gripping her arm just above her elbow, he hauled her to her feet, swinging the rucksack over his other shoulder. "We have to get out of here."

Sabine strained to see the burning helicopter. "Are we going to—"

"They're dead," he cut her off.

Tears pushed into her eyes. "Oh—my God… I'm so sorry."

He didn't respond, just pulled her along. With a will of iron that had seen her through two weeks of unimaginable suffering, she forced her tears away. She stumbled and fell against Rudy, nearly falling. Her legs wouldn't support her very much longer. She was amazed she could walk at all.

Rudy muttered a curse and hefted her over his shoulder again. She bit her lip against the stab of pain in her ribs. The glowing orb of the helicopter disappeared from view as Rudy walked. His strides grew monotonous. She had no concept of passing time.

When Rudy finally eased her from his shoulder, she groaned as she lay on the ground. Her entire body throbbed. She tried not to vent her discomfort with audible sounds. Rudy had enough to worry about. And she wanted him to get her out of there.

She saw him dig into his rucksack and pull out a handheld radio. He lifted it to his mouth and depressed a button with his thumb.

"Dasher, this is Rudy. Do you read?"

The names he'd called his teammates penetrated her awareness. Comet. Blitz. Was that short for Blitzen? Now Dasher. Was Rudy short for Rudolf? Was that his code name?

"Dasher, come in." There was a short crackling noise followed by nothing.

Rudy wiped his forehead with the back of his hand.

The radio crackled. "Rudy, this is Dasher. I read you. What happened? Over." The radio crackled again.

"I'm going to set a flare. You have to get here before anyone else finds us. Over."

"I don't see any movement near the crash sight. I'll find you. Over."

"Hurry." Rudy tossed the radio into the rucksack and dug for something else. He stood when he found the flare and moved away from Sabine a few steps. He was efficient and fast with his hands as he lit the flare and sent it into the night sky.

Sabine watched the flare illuminate the landscape. She could see nothing that suggested anyone was after them, but she rubbed her arms anyway, afraid of the possibility, so afraid. She would not survive if she had to face more torture. Not after tasting freedom again.

Her gaze shifted to Rudy. He stood with his feet slightly parted, searching the landscape. Only then did she notice he held a pistol at his side.

The sound of a helicopter broke the silence. Rudy tipped his head back and closed his eyes. She felt his relief, and it sparked hope along with a fresh threat of tears. Were they really going to make it?

The helicopter neared. Soon it tossed up dirt as it landed and Rudy helped her to her feet, carrying the rucksack in his other hand. She leaned against him as they made their way to the helicopter, Rudy bearing most of her weight. He boosted her inside and she crawled into the pod. Leaning against the far side, she watched Rudy climb in as the helicopter lifted into the air.

He lay on his back and draped his arm over his forehead, his massive chest rising and falling from more than exertion. Sabine knew he was thinking of his men. Remorse overwhelmed her. It was so unfair.

She folded her arm over her ribs, wishing the pain would ease. She closed her eyes to ride it through. Hearing movement, she opened her eyes and saw Rudy rolling to his hands and knees. He stood and crossed the small space of the helicopter.

Crouching before her, he asked, "How badly are you hurt?"

He must have noticed her holding her ribs. "I'll be all right." As long as she was away from those terrible men, she was fine.

Rudy pulled her arm away from her body. "Is anything broken?"

"I don't think so." She had her big-boned grandfather on her mother's side to thank for that. She'd never met her grandparents on her father's side. "Except maybe my ribs." Her injuries would fade. It was what she'd witnessed that would haunt her the rest of her life. The memory of Samuel.

She winced when he tested her ribs with his hands, unable to suppress a moan.

The furrow between his eyebrows deepened, and he pulled her T-shirt up to her breasts in a purely clinical maneuver. Only the tightening of his mouth revealed anything of his reaction to the expanse of bruises on her torso.

"Did your captors want anything specific?" he asked. "Did you hear any of them talk?"

"We never were told why we were being held," she breathed through the sharp throbs in her ribs.

Dropping her shirt, Rudy stood and moved away.

She watched him reach into the rucksack and pull out a canteen. Wordlessly, he handed it to her along with two pills. She studied him as she took the pills and popped them into her mouth. Next, she took the canteen and lifted it to her mouth with an unsteady hand. He seemed to notice and crouched in front of her again. His hand covered hers as he helped her hold the canteen. She met his eyes while she drank, the striking gray of them momentarily capturing her. He didn't have his helmet on anymore, and she realized she didn't remember when he'd removed it. He had thick, dark hair. Something about it struck her as odd. Didn't military men have close-cropped hair?

She wiped her mouth after she finished drinking, and he took the canteen from her.

"Who would want to keep you from leaving this place?" he asked.

The question gave her a jolt. Did he wonder if it could be someone other than her kidnappers? "I don't know."

"Someone must have. And it wasn't your captors."

She took a moment to absorb that. If not her captors, who would want her to die like that? Had they known she and Samuel were being held? And done nothing? Everything inside her rebelled against the idea. It was too awful.

"That helicopter wasn't in any of the images I saw," Rudy continued, his mouth a tight line of anger. "They knew we were coming." And that missing piece of information had cost him three good men.

Who would go to such lengths to see her and Samuel dead? She didn't have any enemies like that. Her father, but he had no reason to want her brutally killed. And if anyone had the means to orchestrate her rescue, it was he. She glanced at Rudy's longish hair.

"Who sent you here?" she asked more briskly than she intended. "Who are you?"

His anger disappeared behind a guarded mask. He unfolded his legs to stand. "I'm bringing you home. That's all you need to know."

"Was it my father?" she asked anyway.

"No." He turned away and went toward the cockpit of the helicopter, ending any further questioning.

Dust billowed into the air and the whine of engines drowned any other sound. Sabine hooked her arm over Rudy's shoulder as he carried her to a waiting plane. The airstrip was crude and deserted. The plane was painted white with a horizontal blue stripe and no other markings. Rudy climbed some steps and took her inside. There were no seats and darkness filled the row of windows. He put her down and she sat on the floor, leaning against another metal-sided wall.

Rudy turned to speak to Dasher, who was apparently an accomplished pilot, since not only had he flown the helicopter, but also he was going to fly this plane out of Afghanistan. For the first time in two weeks, she felt her shoulders sag in relief. Soon she'd be home.

Home. That seemed like a foreign place to her now, where everything was normal. She felt anything but normal. She didn't know the woman who'd survived what she had. How was she going to move on as though none of this had ever happened?

Samuel would never go home. He'd never see his wife again. The last conversation she'd had with him would stay with her always.

In the darkness of their cell, they'd talked well into the night. Sleep had been patchy and filled with nightmarish dreams. Like every other night.

Sabine had learned a lot about Samuel in the weeks they'd been held captive. He was steady and family oriented. He loved his wife to the depths of his soul and hated the time he had to be away from her; he wanted to build a house for her and the kids they'd planned to have. It was the reason he'd taken the contracting job.

Dasher headed for the cockpit. Once again, she was alone with the man who'd rescued her.

Rudy closed the door and the whine of the plane's engines increased. He sat at her feet on the floor, leaning against the adjacent wall that divided this compartment from the rear of the plane. With his eyes half closed and his hands resting comfortably in his lap, he had an outward appearance of calm. Hovering alertness. Physical strength at rest but ready to move. And clever gray eyes. He was a dangerous man.

Her father wouldn't have sent any other kind.

Sabine didn't want to believe her father had sent Rudy. She didn't want to owe a man like Noah Page for something as precious as her life, especially after almost losing it because of him. All those years she'd wasted striving to prove she was worthy of his respect had gotten her nowhere. It made her sick to think she'd allowed him to influence her like that, to know that, at least on a subliminal level, she wanted his recognition.

She closed her eyes. No. Her father hadn't sent Rudy. This was a military operation. It had to be. Rudy didn't want to reveal his identity because of the nature of his covert operations and the press her rescue would shake up once word got out that she was on her way home.

Exhaustion overpowered her worry, and she lay on the floor. She woke briefly when they landed for a fuel stop, then again when she felt the plane begin its descent for another. Moments later the tires touched the ground.

The plane slowed until it stopped. Like the last time they'd refueled, the pilot left the plane while Rudy watched from the doorway.

"Where are we?" Sabine asked.

"An airstrip in Egypt," he said without looking at her.

Then his body went rigid as he peered through the door. Sabine pushed herself up to sit.

He looked at her over his shoulder. "Wait here." Then he leaped from the plane.

Sabine crawled to her feet. The crack of gunfire sent her heart skipping faster. Someone was shooting at them again. Who? More gunshots exploded.

She stumbled toward the doorway, searching the plane for a weapon on her way. Seeing Rudy's pistol sticking out of his pack, she slipped it free and leaned against the wall of the plane next to the door, breathing hard from exertion and fear. Peering outside, she spotted Rudy running back toward the plane, a man chasing him with a gun. In the distance, she could see a body lying on the dirt runway.

Forcing her fear down, Sabine lifted the pistol, aimed and fired. The man chasing Rudy dove for the ground, dirt spitting near his feet. Another man appeared in her view and fired at

Rudy. She covered him as best she could, until he leaped into the plane, bumping her shoulder on his way. She stumbled as he slammed the door shut, then pounded it once with his fist.

Bullets hit the door. Sabine jumped back at the loud sound.

He turned and she saw the anger in his eyes before he hurried to the cockpit, his strides long and his feet thudding hard on the metal floor.

She followed, jumping again as bullets hit the plane once more. "Where's Dasher?"

"Dead." Rudy sat in the pilot's seat and worked controls, his face tight with fiery emotion. "They were waiting for us."

Again. How could it have happened again? Who didn't want her to escape her captors?

Sabine clumsily fell into the copilot's seat and fastened the shoulder harness. Darkness stared back at her through the window of the cockpit. The plane rolled down the dirt runway, picking up speed. The sound of bullets hitting metal faded. The plane lifted off the ground.

"Who keeps coming after us?" Who had fired at them in the helicopter, and who was firing at them now?

Rudy didn't answer, his face intense and focused on flying the plane. She let him for a while.

Looking out the window to her side, she saw only darkness. "Where are we going?"

"We have to get to Athens."

She turned her head toward him. "Do we have enough fuel?"

"Probably not," he said, still looking straight ahead and at the controls.

"But…don't we have to fly over the Mediterranean to get to Athens?"

"Yes. And we have to fly low."

Staring through the dark front window, she took several calming breaths. "We're going to die."

Rudy turned his head toward her, his eyes fierce with determination. "Not if I can help it."

As much as she'd have loved to fall into the warmth his energy stirred, Sabine gripped the armrests of her seat and remained tense.

He must have noticed because he said, "There are lots of islands off the coast of Greece. We'll find one and land there if we have to."

Did he actually think they'd find a lovely Greek island and have a nice little landing as if they'd planned it all along? She sat with tight, aching muscles for long, unbearable minutes. Each second felt like her last. At any moment the plane would roar down to the water and it would be over.

"We're getting close," Rudy said at last.

"Really?" She couldn't let herself believe it.

The plane gave her a jolt. The engines cut then roared to life. Cut. Roared.

Her heart thudded sickly in her chest. A lump of fear lodged in her throat.

They were running out of fuel!

"I think I see something," Rudy said.

Sabine strained to see through the night but saw nothing. Was he hallucinating in the face of death? The plane lost elevation as it sputtered along. She gripped the armrests tighter. They were going down. She didn't think she was lucky enough to survive two crashes in one day.

"Do you see it?" Rudy asked. He sounded excited.

She turned to look at him. How could he be enjoying this? He glanced at her and smiled, then jerked his head toward the front of the plane.

Sabine looked there and searched once again for something in the distance. She saw faint lights and panic spiraled out of control.

"We'll never make it!" It was too far.

"We'll make it," he assured her. "All we have to do now is find a place to set this thing down."

"Don't you mean crash it?"

The plane's engines cut and this time died altogether. Rudy guided the plane toward the lights. They were losing elevation fast. Lower. Lower. She could see the surface of the water now. Oh God, they were going to hit!

Instead, the plane whizzed by a rocky shoreline. The shape of a rooftop was next. One of the wings clipped the top of a tree. Rudy tilted the aircraft to one side to avoid another tree, then leveled it as a gently sloping hill appeared below them.

"This is as good as it's going to get."

Sabine squeezed her eyes shut and screamed as the plane struck the ground and bounced and rattled and shook. Her body jerked forward as Rudy worked to bring them to a stop. Loud thunks beneath the plane were the only clue to the kind of terrain they'd landed on. A tree branch smacked Sabine's side of the plane and cracked the front window. The plane slowed. Ahead, she saw the side of a mountain growing larger through the cracked window. The plane slowed to a safer speed but not enough to avoid impact. The crash threw her forward, but the shoulder harness held her body in place. Then she blacked out.

Moaning, she came to and looked around. Rudy was yanking off his harness. He scrambled out of his seat, crouched beside her and held her face in his hand, breathing fast as he inspected her.

"Are you all right?"

She nodded dizzily. "I think so."

He reached for her lap and unfastened her harness. "We have to get out of here and destroy this plane before anyone finds us."

Wasn't it already destroyed enough? She used his sturdy body as leverage and climbed to her feet. Wobbling, she leaned against the side of the plane and waited while he hurried to gather what gear they might need. After he threw a rucksack outside, he helped her through the door. She waited for him there while he set an explosive.

Hooking the rucksack over one arm, he took her hand. "Come on." He led her down the hill, away from the plane.

Sabine stumbled and gripped Rudy's T-shirt to steady herself. When he slowed to a stop, she fell against him.

He dropped the rucksack and put his arm around her. Pulling a black device from his pocket, he depressed a button. A violent explosion followed. Sabine watched as the burning plane lit up the night and gave her a glimpse of rocky peaks surrounding the hilly earth where they had landed.

"Can you walk?"

She looked up at him and nodded, not really all that sure how long she could. But she didn't want him to have to carry her anymore.

Rudy led her the rest of the way down the hill. An hour later, they hiked over a steeper hill. Sabine thought of them as hills because they were nothing like the mountains she grew up in. Southwestern Colorado was filled with fourteen-thousand-foot giants that made these look like foothills.

Her limbs were trembling by the time they crested the peak. Rudy stopped. Sabine hooked her arm with his as she had several times along the way and leaned against him, breathing hard and closing her eyes even though she saw lights at the bottom of the slope that relieved her immensely.

"It's a village," he said, and she heard relief that matched hers and something else. Incredulity at their fortune.

"Where are we?" she asked.

"I don't know. One of the Greek islands."

She turned to study his profile, unable to comprehend how she'd come from a small concrete cell awaiting a horrific death to something as magnificent as a Greek island.

Rudy began walking again, taking her support with him. She collapsed to her hands and knees. A very strange sensation. She had no control over the movement of her legs. Virtually all her strength had abandoned her. Combined with her throbbing and stinging body, she was finished. Her head pounded like lightning strikes with each pulse of her heartbeat.

Rudy cursed. Two strides brought him back to her. He lifted her into his arms, rucksack hanging from one arm, and carried her down the slope. He found a footpath and followed it.

"Don't lie to me when I ask you a question."

She looked up at his rugged face. "I didn't lie."

"You said you could walk."

"I did walk."

He looked down at her beneath a scowling brow.

"You didn't ask how far. We've been walking a long time," she said.

He didn't respond but the scowl remained. Several minutes later they reached the main road going through the village. It was paved but it was the only one that was. No one moved in the street, but it was late at night.

A door opened in a building to their right. An older woman wearing a dark, embroidered dress spoke rapidly in a language Sabine didn't understand. She looked at Rudy when he answered fluently in the same tongue.

He stopped walking and spoke to the woman awhile longer. The woman pointed up the street and spoke again.

Moments later Rudy carried Sabine to a white mortar building with neat rows of square windows lining the first and second floors. At the door, he put her down but kept his arm around her waist for support. She leaned against him while he opened the door, her legs shaking. Inside, a small sitting room with a single light burning on a simple desk illuminated walls covered with row after row of ornately painted plates. Rudy stepped inside with her and closed the door behind them. A short, thin man with dark hair and missing front teeth yawned as he emerged from a dining area, slipping into a robe.

Rudy deposited Sabine onto a chair and spoke to the man, whose name seemed to be Alec. They exchanged words until Rudy finally nodded and handed over a few American bills. Alec handed him a key, and Rudy turned and approached her. She would have protested as he lifted her, but she was so exhausted she didn't think she'd make it three steps.

Their host watched but made no comment as Rudy climbed a narrow stairway. Down a hallway carpeted in a red mosaic pattern, Rudy stopped at a door and put her down on her feet. Her eyes felt heavy and she couldn't wait to lie down on a real bed. Rudy wrapped an arm around her waist and helped her walk inside. Two twin beds on top of a raised platform were covered in white blankets. The walls were adorned with hand-carved lutes and lyres, unique musical instruments that gave a charming clue to the culture of the people here. It was simple but clean and inviting.

Sabine looked to her right and spotted a bathroom. A small sound escaped her. A private bathroom. She tentatively stepped away from Rudy's sturdy support then stumbled toward it. Breathless, she leaned with her hands on the white pedestal sink and saw there was only a small shower. Standing would be a challenge, but she hadn't bathed in two weeks. The thought of a shower charged her with energy she didn't think she had. Determination to be clean fired through her.

Rudy peered into the bathroom, saw the shower with no tub and frowned. "Maybe we should just give you a sponge bath."

Sabine shook her head. "I want a shower."

He turned and met her gaze. Without arguing, he went back into the room and returned with some clothes.

"Leave the door open," he said, and left.

She looked down at the clothes he'd dropped on the floor, wondering where he'd gotten them. Just a white T-shirt, dark blue lounge pants, and underwear, but it would be divine to get out of the clothes she'd been wearing for so long.

"You can sleep in this if you want."

Sabine took the bigger T-shirt he held, watching him go back into the room. He sat in a chair across from the bathroom where he could still see her.

Gripping the edge of the sink with one hand, she pushed the bathroom door with the other until it blocked his view of her, then undressed. She hoped her legs would hold her long enough to get clean. Rudy carrying her the rest of the way to the village had helped some, but what she really needed was rest. Turning on the faucet, she waited for the water to warm before she stepped inside.

Water showered over her head and caressed her battered body. Sabine closed her eyes and moaned. Standing, however, made her legs shake uncontrollably and water trickled into the open wounds on her shins, stinging her. She braced her hands against the shower wall but didn't think it would be enough to keep her upright. When she tried to turn in the shower, her knees gave and she collapsed. Sitting on her hip with her hands flat in front of her, she hung her head and let the water spray fall on her.

Hearing a curse, she looked up to find Rudy holding the shower curtain aside, his mouth in a hard line and his eyes fierce with something more than concern.

Chapter 3

Sabine's pulse jumped faster when Rudy stepped fully dressed into the shower. He leaned down and put his hands under her arms, lifting her easily. She didn't want to see in his eyes the purely instinctual male response to holding a naked woman, so she stood there staring at his broad chest, where her hands were spread.

Anchoring her around her waist, he reached for a small container of shampoo and put some on her head. Sabine wearily lifted her hands and began to wash her hair. Her breath came harder with the effort, but it felt so delicious she closed her eyes and let her head fall back a bit, bringing it more under the spray. She tried not to think about Rudy watching her.

His wet T-shirt heightened her awareness of her body against him. Hard muscle compressed her soft breasts. After she rinsed her hair, he reached behind her and retrieved a bar of soap. Readjusting his hold to support her with one of his powerful arms, he began to wash her back. It felt too good to stop him. She let her head fall to his wet T-shirt-covered chest.

"Turn around."

He sounded raspy. Sabine lifted her head and found her eyes trapped by his unreadable ones. She moved her legs but wouldn't have been able to turn on her own without falling. Now with her back against him, she took the bar of soap and moved it over her skin. She lost herself to the pleasure of feeling clean again. When she finished, she was shaking and short of breath.

Shutting off the water, Rudy lifted her dripping wet in his arms. Sabine pulled a towel from a rack above the toilet when he stopped there and held it to her body as he carried her out of the bathroom. In the other room, he sat in the chair and draped her legs over his. Sabine dried herself on his lap.

"Lean forward," he said, taking the towel from her.

She did and froze. Beneath her, a hard ridge told her just how much the shower had affected him. Seeming not to notice her sudden change, he wrapped her hair in the towel. Then he cradled her, stood and put her back onto the chair, by herself.

Slumping against the chair, she watched him go into the bathroom for the big T-shirt and return. His expression was stern as he gripped the shirt in his hands and pulled it over her towel-covered head. A couple of unceremonious yanks, and the top fell down over her body.

"Thank you," she murmured, glad to be covered again.

He said nothing in response and just lifted her and took her to one of the twin beds, where he'd already pulled the covers down. Before covering her with those, he opened the rucksack and pulled out a roll of bandages and a tube of ointment.

Propped by two fluffy pillows, she shut her eyes and bit her lower lip to keep from crying out when the ointment touched the raw flesh of her shins. Her fingers gripped the sheet and blankets while he wrapped her legs. When he finished, her legs were throbbing so much her mind swam with pain and dizziness.

"I'm sorry," Rudy said.

She couldn't respond with more than a single nod.

He left her and went into the bathroom with the rucksack. When he returned, he was shirtless and in a pair of lounge pants. Sabine caught his profile as he passed the bed and couldn't look away from his broad back. Hard muscles tapered to a trim, fit waist. His butt was tight and perfectly shaped. She held her breath when he leaned over the table and retrieved a bottle of water. Opening it, he faced her and sat on one of the chairs with a long sigh. Lifting the bottle of water he held, he drained half its contents. Sabine forgot the stinging pain in her legs. Smooth skin and a light covering of hair followed the rippling muscles of his chest and abdomen. He sat with his knees spread and his big body slouched lazily in the chair. It gave her a shock to notice him like this, a man with overpowering masculinity that appealed to her on a level she had never experienced.

He lowered the bottle and she stared at his big hand. His other hand lay over the opposite arm of the chair. Those hands had touched her in the shower. Heat began to stir in her. She raised her eyes. He watched her. There was something erotic in his gaze. Leashed interest. Maybe even unwanted desire.

The first shiver of something other than fear raised bumps on her arms. She was alone with him on a Greek island. What would tomorrow be like, she wondered, waking to the Aegean Sea and this mysterious man who'd saved her life?

Cullen sipped a cup of strong Greek coffee and looked out across the turquoise waters of the Aegean Sea. Of all the places to crash-land a DeHavilland, this had to be the best. Under any other circumstances, he'd have enjoyed it. He'd known this rescue would be among the most dangerous he'd ever done, and he'd taken as few men as he could to avoid risking more lives than necessary, but no one should have died. That helicopter had been waiting for them. Anger simmered close to a boil inside him. Only someone close to Noah could have leaked their plans.

He'd give Noah every resource he had to find out who and why, and whoever was responsible would pay with their lives.

Hearing a sound, he glanced at the door of the room. He couldn't see her but knew Sabine had moved on the bed. She'd slept on and off for two days now. He'd decided to let her and had only disturbed her to make sure she drank water and ate and had clean bandages. Letting her sleep this long made him nervous, but it would be better if she could board a commercial plane without drawing too much attention. If he had to carry her, she'd attract attention.

"Hello up there," a woman called in Dorian Greek from below the balcony.

Cullen dropped his feet from the railing and leaned forward to see her better, sending her an answering smile. It was the same woman who'd told him where to find this pension and an available room to rent. Today she wore a white embroidered dress with gold coins draped around her neck. She was a nice enough lady, but she was way too curious about him and Sabine. All it would take was an awestruck villager like her to pick up the phone and talk to the press. The thought nearly made him break into a cold sweat. All he needed was the media to catch up to them.

The woman lifted a basket. "*Makarounes* for you and your lady."

He kept his smile in place as he straightened. "I'll come down."

He turned before she could respond and moved through the room, checking on Sabine before he left her still sleeping. He made his way to the lower level. The pension owner, Alec, looked up and smiled with a nod.

"Good morning," Cullen said in Greek, and Alec answered in kind.

The wrinkled woman stood outside the door of the pension and smiled when he appeared in the doorway. She extended the basket, its contents wrapped in a red cloth. He took it from her.

"Thank you," he said.

She nodded graciously. "You must bring your lady to my taverna when she is rested. We have fresh seafood every night, and it is very quiet." Her dark eyes held a secretive glint.

The notion of having a romantic dinner with Sabine tantalized him too much for his comfort. "We just might have to take you up on that," he said anyway.

"Alec told me about your crash, and that you were on your honeymoon. You come. Have dinner at my taverna." She told him where it was.

Cullen said nothing. She was just an old woman swept up by the intrigue of a plane crash and the couple who'd survived it. Alec had questioned Cullen on the crashed airplane, and Cullen had come up with the quickest explanation he could think of without revealing his and Sabine's identities. They'd come to Greece on their honeymoon and crashed before they'd reached Athens.

The woman waved and turned to go. Cullen squinted as he leaned his head out the door and caught rays of sunlight, watching her walk down the narrow street.

He wasn't sure why being known as a newlywed bothered him. Maybe it was the shower, and Sabine's determination to see it done. The woman had grit. She also had a body made for his hands and eyes that beckoned with green fire. She flared an instinctual response in him. The degree of his interest made him nervous. He liked his relationships comfortable, not out of control. He didn't need that kind of intensity with a woman. His job gave him plenty of that. If he ever got married, it'd be to Mrs. Compatible and Good in Bed, not Mrs. Take My Heart and

Twist It into a Pretzel of Agonizing Love. He'd seen what that could do to a man.

Back in the room, Sabine was as he'd left her, rumpled covers enveloping her, red hair tangled over the pillow. She looked very snug and content. He didn't want to explore the other "verys" he thought she was. *Knew* she was, now that he'd seen her naked.

Taking the basket out to the balcony, he set it on the table. At almost eleven, it was close to lunch.

An hour passed before he heard the sound of Sabine stirring inside the room again. He listened to the toilet flush, and moments later her bare feet trudged toward the balcony. He started to rise to help her but stopped when he saw that she was moving all right on her own, limping but all right. The T-shirt fell to just above her knees, exposing the bandages he'd wrapped around her tender shins. Her legs were skinny but spectacular. He bet they'd look even better once she healed and put on some weight. Just like the rest of her.

Cullen raised his gaze to her face as she looked across the Aegean Sea. Her mouth was slightly parted and her green eyes were the brightest he'd seen them since getting her out of Afghanistan. Their whites were healthy and the green color sparkled in the Mediterranean sunlight. The swelling on her lip had gone down, and the cut on her cheek was healing, though bruises still colored her skin and would for a while. She'd used the comb he'd bought in the village. Her hair was naturally curly, but it looked like soft, woven silk and fell to the top of her breasts. Even skinny, she was an extremely beautiful woman. All Irish with smooth, pale skin and striking features. Especially her eyes.

"Where are we?" she asked without looking at him.

He was glad she hadn't noticed his scrutiny. "A village called Olympos. The north end of Kárpathos. It's near Crete."

"Wow."

Cullen had experienced a similar reaction, despite his constant vigilance for someone with a camera or a gun.

He caught her furtive glance when she became aware of him watching her. She sat and reached for one of the bottles of water on the table, careful not to look at him. He had to agree it was strange being in a place like this with someone he'd just rescued. Especially at the cost of his team, the few that he'd dared bring on this mission.

The reminder of what he'd lost punched him again. Nothing had gone according to plan. Who had betrayed their mission and why? None of the men he'd hired were married, but the pilot and medic had parents Cullen would have to face when he returned to the States. He wasn't looking forward to that, especially since he was going to have to lie about where their sons had died.

Sabine's reaching for the basket diverted his attention. He welcomed it and watched her.

She glanced from the basket to him in question.

"Homemade pasta with cheese and onions. A local favorite."

"Mmm." She parted the cloth and lifted the ceramic bowl covered with a matching lid. Next came the bread.

"They make their own bread in outdoor ovens. You can smell it every once in a while." The appeal of this place had penetrated his vigil more than once. But then, he'd always liked Greece.

"Mmm," she murmured again, finding a plastic fork and starting to dig into the pasta.

It disturbed him how much he liked watching her. Her vibrancy. The look in her eyes, as if everything were new to her now.

When she sighed and put the bowl back into the basket, he knew she was full. She'd eaten less than half the *makarounes* and bread.

"How do you feel?"

She nodded, looking at the sea. "Better."

A moment passed with only the sound of waves washing ashore in the distance.

"I want to walk down to the ocean," she announced.

"Now?"

She nodded with a look of pure bliss on her face. How could he deny her after what she'd been through? "Are you sure you're up for that?" It wasn't far, but it would take a good hike to get there.

A smile spread on her face. The transformation hit him like a fist to the gut.

Then those green eyes so full of new life met his. "I want to walk on a beach. I really do."

Cullen struggled with the inclination to do anything she asked as long as she kept smiling like that. The feeling was a bit too strong for his liking. But a walk on the beach wouldn't hurt. "Okay. I went down there while you were asleep. There's a small beach down the hill from here." Secluded and easy to watch for anyone pointing a gun, too. He could plug them off the hillside if they tried to come after them. He ignored the fleeting thought that instead of going to the beach he should get a cab so they could leave the island that afternoon.

Sabine went into the bathroom to change. While she was in there, he stuffed a pistol good for a thousand yards in the waist of his jeans, letting his short-sleeved shirt hang over to conceal it. Then he waited for her at the door. She emerged in the dark blue lounge pants and long-sleeved white henley shirt he'd brought for her. The outfit would cover her bruises. He led her down the narrow stairs to the first floor of the pension. No one was in the sitting area of the entry.

Outside, Cullen watched Sabine for signs of fatigue. She started to breathe heavier as they walked down the street. At the footpath he'd discovered yesterday, he stopped.

"It's a steep descent."

"I'm fine," she said, dismissing him to gimp down the footpath on her own.

Impressed by her courage and spunk, Cullen followed. He caught himself looking at her butt as she moved down the hill and had to force his gaze elsewhere. Rocks and brush painted the hillside, ending where a sandy inlet sloped into the ocean. Gentle waves lapped the shore, the only sound to be heard other than their footsteps.

"Oh," Sabine breathed.

He stepped down the last of the incline, and his booted feet sank into fine, white sand. She was like a painting now. Hair sailing in a slight breeze, eyes full of appreciation that might not have been as profound had she not come so close to losing her life.

She sat on the sand and removed her hiking boots and socks. Then she rolled the hem of her lounge pants to the edge of her bandages, just above her ankles. Rising, she walked to the shore and went into the water, but only far enough to get her feet wet. That salt water would hurt her raw wounds like a thousand bee stings. Cullen removed his boots and rolled his pants up to follow her.

Waves splashed against rocks and crawled over the sand. Offshore, the water was so clear it looked like pool water, glittering, translucent cerulean fading to deep sea.

"Have you ever been to Greece before?" she asked.

"Many times," he answered. "But never here. I've been to Santorini and Athens."

"You speak the language like you're from here."

"My grandmother was born here." It caught him off guard how easily that came from his mouth, personal information he usually never divulged.

"You're Greek?" She gave him a survey, as though confirming it with her eyes.

"Partly. My mother married an Irishman. I had a knack for languages in college."

"What was your major in college?"

"Political science."

"What did you do after that?"

He just looked at her, knowing her questions were deliberate. He couldn't tell her much about himself, particularly what he did after college. Not when a media frenzy awaited her return. Public curiosity would leave his company—which didn't overtly exist and never could—too vulnerable.

"Did you join the military?" she asked.

"Something like that."

Her mouth pursed and she stopped strolling through the water. "What's your name? You can at least tell me that much."

He stopped, too, and faced her. "Rudy."

"That's a stupid name. Even for a code name. Tell me your real name."

He wanted to, and that heightened his concern. "Sabine…"

Pivoting, she resumed her walk through the water, her steps not as smooth as before, frustration giving her verve even as she limped. But that only managed to intrigue him more.

He caught up with her, noticing the subtle jostle of her breasts.

"I'm sure you know everything about me," she said bitterly.

"I know your name is Sabine O'Clery and you're thirty-three years old. Not married, no kids. I know you're from Colorado and for some reason took the contractor job in Afghanistan." He knew more but now was not the time to tell her.

She glanced at him. "I speak Farsi. There was a need for people like me there. I liked the idea of contract work because it gave me an opportunity to make more money and see interesting places." She grunted her laugh. "At the time it seemed like a good idea." Her face grew haunted and she stopped walking, staring out to sea.

"I'm sorry." And he was, for putting that haunted look in her eyes.

Slowly, she turned and lifted her eyes. "How old are you?"

No harm in telling her that. "Thirty-five." When she continued to look at him with those brilliant green eyes, he added, "Not married. No kids."

"That sort of thing is hard for a man in your line of work, isn't it? Having a family, I mean."

He didn't reply, wondering if she was trying to pry more from him. He couldn't let her. He'd already said too much.

"How many of these missions do you do a year, anyway?"

Still, he didn't say anything.

"Who do you work for?"

That especially was off-limits.

Anger flared in her eyes. He marveled at the intensity and couldn't stop himself from looking down when she folded her arms in front of her.

"Is it my father?" She all but spat the last word.

"No."

Her eyes narrowed and he felt dissected as she searched for signs that he was lying. She wouldn't find any. He could pass any polygraph without flinching.

"Then it has to be the military."

He just looked at her. Let her assume he worked for the military. It wasn't completely a lie.

With a frustrated spin, she turned and limped to her boots.

He followed. "Do you have something against your father? Who is he?"

She sat on the sand and started to put on her socks, agitation showing in her movements. "I'm grateful you saved my life. And I'm sorry your teammates were killed."

The memory of his teammates kept him from pressing her for an answer. Instead, he sat beside her, studying her fiery profile. Whatever had estranged her from her father, it must have something to do with the secrets Noah had to keep. She definitely didn't like secrets. But he couldn't let that stop him from keeping some of his own from her. What he did through his company was so black not even his commander in the army reserves knew the truth. If the media got hold of that, it would destroy him.

Sighing, he looked out to sea. He and Sabine were way too curious of each other.

"You probably like not telling me your name," Sabine said without looking up from her boots.

He observed her for a moment, her words sinking in, confirming what he'd already guessed. The curiosity that could mushroom into more if he wasn't careful.

"You don't need to know anything about me," he said as gently as he could. "As soon as I get you to London, you'll never see me again."

She stopped yanking the laces of her boots to look at him in surprise. "You're taking me to London? What happens when we get there?"

He didn't answer. Instead, he started to put on his boots.

Sabine grunted and jerked the laces of her second boot together.

Best thing would be if they could just get along until he got her to London. He didn't want her to bolt because he reminded her of Noah. "Why don't we forget how we got here and just enjoy the island? We might not ever get a chance to come to a place like this again. I say we find somewhere to have dinner tonight. Something local, with fresh seafood."

Deeper anger furrowed her brow. "What would we talk about, Mr. Thirty-Five, Not Married, No Kids?"

He supposed he should have expected her to react like that. And what was he thinking, suggesting they have dinner together?

"I told you I went to college," he said. "You know about my grandmother, too. That's a lot more than most people know."

"Am I supposed to be flattered?"

He had to get a grip on this. Fast. "Sabine, what I do for a living won't survive the kind of publicity your kidnapping is getting. Imagine what your rescue is going to do. As soon as you land in the United States, it's going to be a circus. I can't be seen with you after this. Can't you understand that?"

She didn't reply and struggled to her feet.

Cullen finished with his boots and followed her up the footpath. She was breathing hard climbing the steep slope. Her grimaces and awkward steps told him her legs were hurting.

He started to reach for her.

She swatted his hands away and propelled herself faster up the hill, no doubt on sheer will, casting him a dagger look over her shoulder.

He almost chuckled. One thing was for sure—she was definitely getting better.

Sitting on one of the woven chairs on the balcony, Sabine wondered what had made her so angry earlier. If Rudy didn't want to tell her his name, he didn't have to. Right?

She could hear him moving in the room. The shower started to run. She tried not to picture him in there, but it was impossible after seeing him without a shirt. She didn't want to be attracted to a man who was just like her father.

She tapped the tabletop with her fingers. She wasn't sure what bothered her more—not knowing who'd sent him, or his secrecy. If her father had sent him, that made Rudy a mercenary. A ruthless killer with no loyalty to country or ideals. That notion wrestled with the honorable act of rescuing her, and a niggling inner voice taunted that she didn't know for sure her father's company was that disreputable. But Rudy was keeping things from her and doing it with ease. She hated that in men. Plus, he'd gotten a thrill crash-landing the plane. That in and of itself was a big enough warning sign. The man probably never enjoyed an idle moment.

The shower turned off. Sabine looked toward the room, unable to see him and upset that she wanted to. She heard the bathroom door open. Then Rudy appeared in the doorway in black jeans and a white short-sleeved dress shirt, gray-eyed and tall and dark and too gorgeous to be good for her.

"I'll be right back," he said.

He was probably going on another of his patrols. She nodded.

"Don't go anywhere and keep the door shut, okay?" he added.

"I'll wait here for you," she said. Why did that sound so intimate? Waiting for him. She was going to *wait* for him. And then what?

Her gaze collided with his for a long moment before he turned and left the room.

Sabine put her elbow on the table and propped her chin in her hand, looking over rooftops at the sea in the distance. The smell of baking bread reached her. She inhaled and welcomed the distraction. Below, the street bustled with activity. People riding or leading donkeys passed. Taxis drove by. She could hear the collective chatter from people sitting on a patio at a restaurant up the street.

She got lost in the pleasure of just experiencing the moment, listening to the sounds, smelling the smells, feeling the warm sun on her skin. Living. It lulled her into a doze. She leaned her head back and let the peace take her.

A while later, she had no idea how long, she heard the room door open and close. Rudy emerged onto the balcony and put a bag on the table in front of her.

Wariness mingled with delight. A present, but it was from him. "What's this?"

He seemed reluctant to answer. "For tonight. You can't wear what you have on."

A responding flutter tickled her before she could stop it. What was he doing? He didn't seem to know himself, the heat in his eyes at odds with his shift in weight from one foot to the other.

Flustered, Sabine turned to the bag and reached inside. She lifted a swath of soft white material, holding up the bodice of a dress. It was long sleeved with a scooped neckline. Standing, she faced Rudy. The flowing hem fell to her ankles and would cover her bandages.

"It's like I said earlier—we're here on this island, why not enjoy it?" He sounded defensive, as though he didn't want her to know he had other reasons for picking out this dress.

She smiled to cover the much more serious wave of pleasure that realization stirred. "If you're trying to get my mind off Afghanistan, you're doing a great job."

Chapter 4

All the while she showered and primped in front of the mirror, Sabine wondered if having dinner with Rudy was such a good idea. Granted, they had to eat, and this was Greece, but he'd made it clear she'd never see him again after he sent her on her way to the United States. Did she want to risk exploring something romantic with him? Because with all his secrets, he would be a risk. She'd dated a few men and slept with them, but this wasn't the same. Being with those men had felt comfortable. Being with Rudy set sparks on fire. Big difference.

She inhaled and blew out the air through pursed lips. As long as she kept Rudy's true purpose in mind, she'd be all right. He had rescued her. When he completed his mission, he'd go his way and she'd go hers. Dinner with him would be just that. Dinner. She'd go to taste the local fare, and tomorrow she'd be on her way home.

She left the bathroom and stopped. Rudy sat in a chair by the bed, reading a brochure of some sort. He looked up and went still when he saw her. His gaze slowly devoured her as he rose to stand.

"Are you ready to go?" she asked, doing her best to hide how awkward she felt.

"I knew that dress would look beautiful on you," he said as though he hadn't heard her.

The compliment rushed through her in a warm wave. Just dinner, she told her heart. Stop letting nice arms and abs get in the way.

Seeming to catch himself, he went to the door and waited for her there. She reached the open threshold.

"By the way, we're on our honeymoon," he said.

She stopped abruptly, unable to keep her head from snapping over and up to look at his face.

"If anyone questions us, that's what you tell them," he explained. "For cover."

Embarrassed that she hadn't immediately caught on to that, she left the room, letting him follow down the hall and stairs. In the lobby, Alec looked up from a paper he was reading and smiled.

"I am happy to see you are feeling better, Mrs. Harvey," he said in accented English.

Sabine forced a smile. "Thank you. I do feel much better." She avoided any connection with Rudy's eyes as they left the pension. *Mrs. Harvey. Mrs.*

The sun was low in the sky as they made their way down the street. Rudy led her into an alley. It was so narrow that he had to move behind her to allow a man leading a donkey to pass. Through another alley, they dodged two more people with donkeys and emerged onto a street where a white building with tables outside came into view. Theodosia's, a sign read on the glass door.

Rudy opened the door for Sabine and she entered. The interior was longer than it was wide, with windows along the back that had a view of a rocky shoreline. Dark wood tables with white table-cloths and miniature vases of white flowers filled the space between. The hum of conversation joined the clang of dishes, and the smell was divine. Sabine inhaled a full breath to savor it for a while.

Rudy leaned close. "It's called a *psarotavérna*. A taverna that serves fish."

"It smells like heaven."

"Welcome, welcome." The woman they'd first seen when they'd arrived in the village came forward, her wrinkled face smiling. She wore a red embroidered dress with gold chains hanging from her neck. Her hair was white and in a bun.

"This must be your lovely wife." The woman hooked her arm with Sabine's. "I am Theodosia," the woman said, leading them past tables of Greek-speaking patrons.

At a table in the corner, intimate and lit with a candle, Theo-dosia let go of Sabine, who sat and watched Rudy do the same across from her.

"Enjoy," Theodosia beamed.

Rudy said something in Greek that made her smile wider and laugh as she turned away.

"She's very friendly," Sabine commented.

Rudy scowled. "Too friendly. Maybe we should have gone somewhere else."

"We're the Harveys, remember?" She laughed a little, begin-ning to enjoy this.

He grunted and turned to the menu.

The tension on his face dimmed her playfulness. Did he regret bringing her here? Why had he taken the chance? She was afraid to guess. Why had she agreed to go with him? The answer sobered her. They were both too interested in each other.

A waitress arrived at their table and filled two glasses of water. "You ready, no?"

Rudy ordered. Sabine didn't understand a word he said, but when the waitress left the table, she assumed he'd ordered for both of them.

"What are we having?" she asked.

"Octopus pilaf."

He grinned at her questioning expression, all his tension evaporating.

"Never had it?" he asked.

She smiled and both felt and saw him notice. "No, but I love seafood."

"Me, too." He looked at her in a way that she shouldn't have liked, but oh, how she liked it. The heat and vitality of him warmed her.

One glass of wine arrived at the table. The waitress put it in front of her.

"Aren't you having any?" she asked Rudy when the waitress left.

He shook his head. "I don't drink."

The way he said it made her wonder. "Because your job requires it?"

"No. When you grow up with a drunk for a father, alcohol loses its appeal."

She lifted the glass of wine and sipped, thinking he had not meant to reveal so much feeling and not wanting to let on that she'd noticed. "Where is your father now?"

He met her gaze as she lowered the glass. At first, she didn't think he was going to answer, but it turned out there was too much emotion simmering in him.

"He lives in a low-income housing project with his crack-smoking girlfriend," he said, his tone laced with bitterness and sarcasm.

"Do you ever see him?" she asked, keeping her tone unassuming.

"No. I gave that up the day I left home, when I was sixteen."

"How do you know he has a girlfriend, then?"

"Every now and then I give in to the hope that he's changed and call."

Sabine met his gaze for a while. It hurt him to see his father like that. Had his upbringing motivated him to do what he did for a living? Maybe if he saved enough people, he could make up for not being able to save his father.

"My mother died when I was very young. He never got over it," Rudy added.

"He must have loved her very much."

"Too much. It's what destroyed him."

Sabine covered her inward response with another sip of wine. Maybe that's what had turned him into an adrenaline junky. He didn't want to end up like his father. What better way to accomplish that than always being on the go? Never home. Avoiding relationships that would make him feel too much.

She wondered if her father had had a similar experience that had turned him against commitment to a woman. When she realized she didn't know anything about his childhood, a spark of anger pushed the soft thought aside.

"Is that why you do what you do?" she asked a little harsher than she intended. "Do you feel safer when you conquer and control?"

"My father was a bad role model, and I was never close to him. Luckily, I had an uncle who cared what happened to me. He's the reason I do what I do."

His answer nipped her anger short. She hadn't expected him to reveal yet another detail about himself. Curiosity won over her defenses. "Your uncle is like a father to you?"

Pride and love softened his magnificent eyes. "He's an amazing man. Well liked by everyone, both in his hometown and in the military, even though he's retired. He taught me the importance of standing up for values. For country. For freedom. Fighting for what you believe in. Honor. Humanity. Integrity. All that. He retired a good man with a stellar reputation. I want that. I want to be able to look back on my life when I'm an old man and not feel like I could have done more."

"So your uncle was in the military." And so was he, if she understood his meaning. She didn't want to acknowledge it could be true, that he was nothing like her father. It would be too much of a risk, allowing herself to believe she could trust a man like him. Someone with secrets.

Instead of responding, his eyes went blank, the window to the man inside shut tight. Now that, she thought resentfully, was exactly like her father.

"Did my father hire you?" she asked.

"What kind of man would your father hire?" he answered with a question.

She let him get away with it. "Murderers. Men with no conscience."

"Is that how you think of your father?"

"It's what he is."

"A murderer."

She didn't reply.

"What does he do?"

"Don't you already know?"

He waited.

"He owns a private military company. He loves the thrill. The danger of going into a third-world country for the sole purpose of killing, teaching others to kill, and pilfering the civilization while he's at it."

"You know an awful lot about him for someone who grew up fatherless."

Catching the meaning of his leading comment—that maybe she was exaggerating the truth out of spite—she said, "My mother told me about him when I asked."

"She told you he was a mercenary?"

"He was."

"Pilfering and killing."

She turned her head away, unable to deny emotion might be clouding her judgment.

"I know what it's like to grow up with a parent you feel doesn't love you," he said, bringing her gaze back to him. "So I suppose I can't blame you for the way you feel."

"I didn't grow up with my father around. My mother raised me. The great Noah Page came around often enough, but only for sex. My mother wanted more. He promised more every time, but in the end he always left. He was incapable of loving one woman, giving his whole heart to her. And the thrill of his job was always more important."

Rudy lifted his glass of water and drank, watching her over its rim.

"Does that sound familiar?" she taunted.

He lowered the glass of water. "Are you asking if I'm incapable of loving only one woman?"

He must know she wasn't, but she decided to play along. "Are you?"

"I don't know. I've never been in love."

"Do you want to be?"

His gaze intensified, not letting hers go and reaching deep into her, infusing her with the growing strength of their attraction. "She'd have to be one hell of a woman, Ms. Hydrogeologist Who Went to Afghanistan to Make More Money and See Interesting Places."

The sting of his reply ricocheted through her. His meaning was too clear. To all appearances, she went for thrills just like him and her father.

But until her kidnapping, she'd been living a lie. She'd been living to please others. And judging by Rudy's remark, he liked that she seemed to be a thrill chaser. Would he still hold her in such high esteem if he knew she wasn't that woman anymore? That Afghanistan had ripped her eyes open so she could finally see and accept the truth? She didn't know what she was going to do with her life now. She just had to find herself again, the part of her buried beneath years of identifying herself through achievements.

Upset, she turned her head and looked out the panel of windows along the rear of the taverna.

Rudy's hand slid over hers on the tabletop. Sabine looked down at his masculine hand covering hers.

"I'm sorry," he said.

She raised her eyes. "For what?"

"For putting that look in your eyes."

The gruff sound of his voice set off warnings in her head. If this night lasted too long, she wasn't sure she could resist wherever it led.

Rudy paid for their dinner, and the walk back to the pension was charged with unspoken tension.

Dim light from a paraffin lamp reflected on the knife blade. Then shiny metal grew bloody, spreading as if through soaked cotton. She closed her eyes. A man standing guard over her pummeled the butt of his rifle against her head.

"Open your eyes!" he shouted in the language she now detested.

She opened her eyes. The guard gripped her chin and jerked her head toward the wooden table where Samuel lay tied and writhing. She wailed and shut her eyes.

"Open your eyes!" the guard shouted louder.

She couldn't.

Samuel screamed in pain and she screamed with him. Another blow to her head made her dizzy. She opened her eyes.

The scene blurred. Mercy. But not for long. The monster was near.

She watched, terror a frenzy of incomprehensible energy, a.

a wiry man with short dark hair turned from his victim and faced her, a leer on his mouth and evil raging in his eyes....

Sabine sprang up in bed, staring through the darkness. The dream had been so vivid. She could see that room where Samuel had been tied. Heard his cries of agony all over again. She didn't want to remember, but the images hung in her conscience, awful and tearing. Bringing her knees up, she let her head fall there and cried. Once she started, she couldn't stop.

On the bed next to hers, Rudy stirred. He rose to stand and stepped over to her. Pulling the covers over her legs aside, he sat on the mattress and gently lifted her onto his lap. It was a smooth motion that accompanied the swell of desperate need pumping through her heart. She curled against him, shaken, disoriented. Lost. He offered her comfort and she took it.

She cried until she felt drained and empty. So empty. How was she going to find her way through the foreign landscape of her soul? How would she ever learn to live with the torture of her memory? She just wanted to forget.

"Do you want to talk about it?" Rudy asked, pulling her from the dregs of torment.

She shook her head, more of a roll against his hard muscled chest. It was too hideous to put into words. Unfathomable. That another human being could do what had been done to Samuel and what would have been done to her.

"You're going to have to at some point."

She raised her head to look at him. His eyes were mellow with caring, plain for her to see. Unguarded. She was seeing all of him right now. Such a gift, this willing exposure of his self. It loosened something inside her. She could forget the horror of her ordeal in his arms. Escape it. Why not let him do that for her?

Impulse made her lean closer, tilt her head. Her lips were a hair's width from his. Just a slight movement closed the distance. A feather touch. She tasted his warm breath. Sweet. Soft.

She moved back a fraction to look up into his eyes. Shadowed and darkly intense, they glowed in the meager light. She kissed him again, this time moving her lips over his to find the best fit. His arm went rigid around her back. She touched his lower lip with her tongue, then gently sucked where it had been, hoping he wouldn't withdraw. He made her feel so good. She needed to feel good again.

Rewarded by the sound of his quickening breaths, she slid her hands up his chest and around his neck. Now her breasts pressed against his hard body. She felt his hand on her thigh. The one on her back didn't move. She touched her lips to his again. His mouth answered hesitantly. She reveled in the intimate contact, the soft brush of their mouths, the gentle play. When he pulled away, she leaned her head back, closing her eyes to feeling.

Rudy kissed her neck, her jaw, the soft spot below her ear. His masculine rasps were erotic in the room. She moved her head and found his mouth again. A sound escaped her as she opened to him, wanting more than a chaste kiss. He reached deep with his tongue. Her injured lip protested against the force of his passion but wasn't enough to make her want to stop him.

His hand moved up her thigh, excruciatingly slow. When he reached the hem of her underwear, he went inside and cupped bare flesh. Heat spread through her, sweet tingles radiating from her core to the ends of her limbs. Their breathing resounded like soft whispers in the room. She pulled away from his mouth to trail kisses down his throat. But she couldn't stay away from that mouth for long and returned for another long, searching kiss. He lifted up her T-shirt. She left his mouth only long enough for him to raise the shirt over her head and toss it aside. Her breasts touched his bare chest when she returned to kissing him.

"Mmm," he murmured, and Sabine knew he'd lost his remaining restraint.

The muscles of his stomach tightened as he rolled onto his hip, making her land with her rear on the mattress. She dropped her arms from his neck to touch his chest. He hooked the hem of her underwear and pulled the garment down her legs. Kneeling between her legs, careful of the bandaged area, he came down to her, gently, without putting weight on her ribs.

She stopped thinking about that when she felt his erection through his underwear. On his elbows, his fingers raked into her hair and he kissed her.

"Tell me your name," she said against his warm mouth.

"Rudy," he said, kissing her again.

"Please," she breathed. "I need…" He rubbed himself against her, and her mind blanked for a second.

Pushing the waistband of his underwear down, she cupped her hands over his butt. His hips moved again, harder this time, and she felt his erection, parting without entering. Her mind blanked again.

He took her open mouth and kissed her hard and deep, still moving against her. He sucked a spot on her neck then dragged his tongue down to her breast. Sabine thought her eyes would roll backward from the sensations firing through her.

"Tell me your real name," she barely managed to say. *She had to know his name.*

His mouth slid off her nipple and moved up her neck until he found her lips. Lifting his head, he looked down at her.

Passion mingled with hesitation.

"Tell me," she urged, lifting her head to kiss him reverently, a tender caress.

He kissed her back then looked down at her again. A long moment passed.

"Cullen."

"Cullen." She looked into his eyes and gave him another

worshipful kiss. "Cullen. Cullen. Cullen." She met his mouth again. When she withdrew, she opened her eyes and found his.

"Make love to me, Cullen."

He kissed her. One soft taste after another, taking his time with it, heating her to mind-numbing rapture. He moved down, grazed her nipple with his tongue, then traced the edge of her bruises before kissing his way down to her stomach. He made her entire body sing with pleasure. Even her toes tingled.

Yes, this is exactly what she needed. To feel alive again. To forget.

Coming back up to her, he looked into her eyes while his hand went down her side, over the curve of her hip, down her leg. Shivers rocketed through her as his fingers caressed the tender flesh of her inner thigh, up, up, until they grazed her wetness. Her breath caught and for a moment she thought she would come apart right then.

"Mmm," he murmured darkly.

Sabine grabbed his wrist, unable to take any more. He met her eyes and seemed to understand. He rose to his knees and she watched him take off his underwear with jerky tugs, his smoldering gaze never leaving her.

He dropped his underwear off the side of the bed and stretched over her, propped by his hands to keep from coming in contact with her bruises. The hard ridge of him rubbed against her warmth. Sabine put her hands on his butt and urged him to do more. He pulled back and the tip of him found her and pushed inside. The delicious pressure of his never-ending length filled her. He groaned and withdrew to push into her again.

Sabine gripped his hard biceps. He stayed above her while he thrust back and forth, strumming unbearable sensation to a crescendo.

A powerful orgasm shook her. It went on and on, a gripping eruption that made her cry out. When the waves subsided, he drove into her with more force, sliding one arm under her waist, tipping her hips and renewing the sizzle. She met his feverish kisses and her moan was deep and raw as she clenched around him a second time. He sank hard into her a few more times before he made a gruff sound and he came down on his elbows, resting his head beside hers. Many moments passed as he lay there on top of her, still inside her but spent.

Peace settled over Sabine. The demons in her mind were far, far away. Where Cullen had pushed them. She was warm and safe and content. When he rolled onto his back, she sighed and curled against him, positioning herself so her ribs didn't hurt. No words were necessary. The peace was enough. Lulled, she slept.

Sabine woke to the sound of ocean waves and the smell of coffee. As she stretched, even her aches and pains didn't penetrate the lovely glow that greeted her.

Finding her big T-shirt, she pulled it over her head before heading toward the open balcony door. She could see Cullen's legs where he sat on one of the chairs. Warmth suffused her with the memory of what he'd done with her the night before. In the open doorway, she stopped. He turned his gaze from the ocean and looked up at her. She smiled.

"We need to leave in an hour."

Her smile vanished along with the lovely glow. Coldness swept into its place. Nothing remained of the gentle and caring man who'd held her and made love to her. He was the purposeful soldier he'd been when he found her in the Panjshir Valley. He was doing his job and she was part of it. Last night had been part of it. Or had it? Why was he so distant this morning? It crashed into her conscience that she already knew the answer.

Chiding herself for letting herself believe, even for a moment, that Cullen would change the course of his mission after one

night, that it would mean enough for him to at least acknowledge what had happened, she turned without comment and went
to get ready. What happened last night had been nothing more
than a therapy session. With that first kiss, she'd asked him for
an outlet to her despair and he'd given her one.

Dressing after a shower, Sabine entered the room and found
him waiting by the door, rucksack at his feet. He watched her
impassively as she approached. To her shame, she couldn't hold
his gaze. She preceded him out the door and discovered he'd
arranged for a car to come and get them. She sat on the opposite
side of the backseat from him and stared out the window all the
way to a small airport on the other side of the island.

She didn't know where he'd attained their passports and
didn't care enough to ask. Asking would require that she speak
to him, and she didn't feel like doing that.

They boarded a plane to Athens. Cullen let her board first and
she sat in the window seat. He made no attempt to talk to her.
The few times she glanced at him, he was as emotionless as he'd
been that morning. But he watched her. In an unnerving way she
was beginning to hate.

In Athens, they had to wait for their flight to London. Sabine
found a chair near their gate and occupied herself studying the
crowd around them. Greek people were beautiful, which only
depressed her further. Cullen was part Greek. He looked Greek.

He gave her a reprieve from his weighty presence and disappeared for a while. When he returned with two coffees, she took
one of them.

He sat beside her. She ignored him but felt his frequent glances.

"You knew it would come to this," he said after a while.

Lowering her cup from the sip she'd just taken, she slid her
gaze to him. "If you're worried about last night, don't be."

"Nothing would have happened if I'd have known you were
expecting more from me."

She faced forward and resumed her people-watching to cover the gouge to her emotions. Hadn't she learned not to expect more from anyone? Every time she'd expected more from her father, she'd always been shot down. Cullen was no different. She reined in her building anger. "Well, I'm not, so you're off the hook."

"I can tell you're upset."

"I'm upset with myself, not you, so don't let it go to your head."

He grunted a short laugh. "You were the one who kissed me."

"You kissed me back."

She heard him sigh, a frustrated sound. "But if I'd have known you were expecting more, I would have stopped."

She hated how he repeated that. "I wasn't. I was just… I wasn't thinking, that's all."

"Me, neither," he said.

She caught his gaze and held it. Had he been as swept away as she? Is that what had made him so distant? She fought the desire to cling to that rationale. It was such a familiar instinct, so like how she'd felt growing up, after each time her father came home, then left her mother broken when he inevitably left.

An announcement came to board their plane. Cullen stood and Sabine followed him onto the plane. He stuffed his rucksack in the upper compartment and sat next to her. She propped her elbow on the armrest and stared out the window. Moments later the plane raced down the runway and they were airborne. It wouldn't be long now. Soon she'd be in London. She'd never see him again.

She tried not to notice how close his thigh was to hers, or his hand on the armrest. The same hand that had touched her so intimately last night. His nearness suffocated her. She could even smell him. It was disconcerting, how her heart had become so tangled with him in such a short period of time.

The plane landed in London and taxied toward the gate. A lump formed in her throat. She didn't even know the man beside her. She knew only his first name and precious few details about him. How could she have feelings for him? It was her ordeal. She was emotional and vulnerable. Any man would have done the trick.

But she knew that wasn't true. Not just any man would have done what Cullen had done for her.

He said nothing as he walked with her through the London airport. When they reached the main terminal and the doors leading to passenger pickup, he slowed, taking her hand to stop her.

Reluctantly, she faced him. He wasn't going any farther with her. She would walk one way and he would walk the other. Her nerves began to fray.

He pulled her toward him. She flattened one hand on his chest as he curved his fingers around the back of her neck.

"I don't regret what happened," he said gruffly.

The sound of his voice, what he said, and the hungry heat in his eyes washed through her. Finally there was the emotion he'd hidden from her all morning. One night together hadn't satisfied him any more than it had her.

His head came down. She felt the featherlight touch of his lips on hers. The same fire that had pulsed between them last night flared to life again. He released her hand and slid his to her lower back. She curled her freed hand over his biceps. Angling his head, he kissed her deeper. Harder. She answered with everything she had in her heart. People moved behind her. The sound of voices and people shuffling by were dim in comparison with the riot of sensation clamoring inside her.

Long seconds later, Cullen lifted his head. She shared a silent moment with him, looking deep into his eyes. Then she touched his face, running her fingers along his jaw and lips. She hadn't imagined the poignancy of last night. He'd felt it, too.

He took her hand in his, kissed it, then lowered it to her side. Letting go, he stepped back.

"There'll be a black Mercedes SUV parked outside. Waiting for you."

Reality intruded. Waiting? She stiffened. "Who?"

"You'll recognize him."

Dread washed through her in one awful wave. If it was her father waiting outside, then Cullen worked for him. Nothing she'd begun to believe about him was true. She stepped backward, watching a kind of resignation creep into his eyes. He had expected this moment to come. Of course she'd suspected her father might have sent him, but finding it true was far more painful. Cullen *was* a mercenary. She'd slept with a mercenary.

She turned and walked with a limp toward the door. There, she couldn't stop herself from one last look. People walked to and fro, taking no notice of him where he still stood near a cement column that concealed him from most angles except behind and in front of him. Hands at his sides, messy dark hair, eyes shadowy and hard, he looked tall and formidable.

She'd never see him again. Part of her screamed not to leave. Pretend he wasn't the kind of man she feared and that it wasn't her father waiting outside this door. If she could just stay in Cullen's arms. Go back to Kárpathos. Keep kissing him and never surface into reality…

But that was impossible. Sabine had no place in Cullen's life. He'd deliberately kept details of her rescue from her, knowing she would not have agreed to go with him to London. Not with her father waiting here. Not knowing her father had arranged everything. Cullen. Her rescue. Everything.

Numbly, she pushed the door open. She stayed in the doorway, frozen by the sight ahead of her. A man stood near the rear passenger door of a Mercedes SUV. It was shiny and black, with windows so dark she couldn't see inside. Her heart turned to ice as she stared at her father.

Noah Page stood with his hands clasped behind him, dark

sunglasses hiding the blue eyes that had so bewitched her mother. His dark hair had grayed, and he'd gained a few more wrinkles since she last saw him, but his tall frame was still fit. A requirement of his profession.

Beside him another man leaned against the front fender of the SUV. The open lapels of his jacket revealed the strap of a harness, telling her he was armed.

She looked once again at her father. She hadn't seen him since the day she graduated from college. He hadn't been invited and must have known she'd resent his presence. Yet he'd come, as though years of neglect and empty promises could be forgotten by such a feeble gesture of interest in her life.

And now he was here, picking her up after one of his henchmen had rescued her. A mercenary on her father's payroll. Cullen, who'd made love to her last night like no other. Cullen, who epitomized the worst kind of man for her. A man who lied to ensure he'd get her here.

She wondered what she would have done had he told her the truth. Maybe she'd known the truth all along. Just hadn't allowed herself to believe it.

Oh, God. Sabine's hand tightened on the door handle. Ever since Cullen had held her in the helicopter, something about him had reached her heart. His heroism. His strength. Everything good in a man…everything she dreamed a man should be.

Still holding the door open, heart racing with a riot of conflicting emotions, Sabine looked behind her. The spot where Cullen had stood was empty.

Chapter 5

Nothing could have prepared Sabine for the welcome home that awaited her in Denver. She could see the throng that had gathered behind a short concrete barrier as her father's business jet came to a halt in front of the jetCenter at Centennial Airport.

"My God," she murmured, staring in awe at the crowd of well-wishers.

"Damn her," Noah cursed from the leather seat beside her. "No one would have known about our arrival if it weren't for her."

Knowing the "her" he referred to was her mother, Sabine turned from the window to glare at him. He'd tried several times on their way to strike up a congenial conversation. More than once she'd caught herself wanting to rejoice that he was showing an interest in her at all, that perhaps she'd finally achieved the ultimate reward and won his respect. But his effort to assume the role of father came too late, and she resented him for having the gall to use her rescue as a means to get close.

"So sorry you're in a bind, Father," she said, moving her gaze back to the scene outside the window. So many people. She had no idea what she would say. Did she have to say anything?

Her father stood and extended his hand. "Come on."

Ignoring his offer of help, she pulled her own weight from the seat and forced him to step back as she made her way to the exit.

Her heart jackhammered as she emerged from the jet. A roar of cheers erupted. Sabine smiled and waved, nervous and happy and confused. She didn't feel deserving of such a grand welcome. All she'd done was survive something terrible.

Her mother materialized from the crowd, running toward the jet. Sabine laughed and cried at the same time as she stepped down the remaining stairs, using the rail for support.

Nothing had ever looked so good as her mother coming toward her with open arms. Mae O'Clery smiled with tears streaming down her face. An active woman of fifty, Mae had retained her shape and kept her hair shoulder-length and dyed red to hide the gray. Sabine limped toward her. Air whooshed out of her when she found herself encased in her mother's arms. The cheers grew louder and clicks from cameras went off everywhere.

"My baby girl." Her mother's pet name for her had always annoyed Sabine because she used it so often. But now it was like music. Sabine cried harder.

"You don't know how happy I am to see you," her mother croaked.

"I think I do," Sabine said. "About as happy as I am to see you."

They laughed through tears.

"Oh." Mae leaned back and touched Sabine's face with both hands, her green eyes moist with tears. "Welcome home, darling."

Her mother's smile faded when her gaze shifted. Sabine watched her wipe her tear-streaked face. Turning, she saw her father standing close, his eyes fixed on Mae with a look of longing.

All the old resentment and uncertainties boiled up, the worry that her mother's love for him would once again blind her into another brief reunion. Then it would be only a matter of time before her father got restless. He'd leave like he always did. And the agony would play its course inside her mother.

"Thank you," Mae said to Noah.

A soft smile formed on his lips, changing his expression to one of affection. "You know I would have done anything to bring her back to you."

"Sabine."

The sound of her name interrupted the animosity building toward her father. She turned and saw Aden Archer come to a stop beside her mother, wearing sunglasses, a hesitant smile flickering on his mouth. His thinning brown hair waved in a slight breeze. He leaned his wiry, average-height frame forward and hugged her.

Sabine felt awkward hugging him back. It seemed so stiff. So forced.

When he moved back, she wanted to take his sunglasses off to see if there was anything telling in his eyes. And there were so many questions she wanted to ask.

"I'm so glad you made it home," he said, and sounded deeply sincere. "I wish I could have done something. If it wasn't for your father…"

"I know." She didn't want to say more, to feel so beholden to her father.

"The papers are saying no one knows why you and Samuel were taken."

She nodded slowly. "That's true." Would she ever be able to

hear Samuel's name without feeling a wave of grief? His body had been found along a village road near where they had worked, her father had told her on the way back to the States. It had been left there as a message, but of what, and by whom?

"You couldn't tell the authorities anything that might help?" Aden's question jarred her from her thoughts. "No leads? Nothing?"

Still thinking of Samuel, she answered more aggressively than she intended. "No. Believe me, if I knew anything, I'd tell them all I could."

He nodded. She wondered if he was as guarded as he seemed. Was he hiding remorse, or something else she couldn't read?

"We should go, Sabine." Her father cupped her elbow and began to lead her away.

Aden stood watching her, a half smile emerging on his mouth. It gave her an eerie chill. She couldn't explain why.

When she couldn't crane her neck to watch him any longer, she faced forward and spotted a dark car waiting. Mae caught up to her and Noah and slipped her arm under Sabine's.

The renewed roar of cheers was deafening. Cameras went off like firecrackers. Security personnel kept the crowd behind the concrete barrier.

"I'm afraid I caused quite a stir," Mae said with a giddy laugh. "I couldn't stop telling people you were coming home today. I'm afraid word got around. I'm sorry."

"Don't worry, Mom."

Noah walked beside Sabine toward the waiting car. If so many people hadn't been watching, she'd have cringed away from his hand on her back.

"Will you tell us about your rescue, Miss O'Clery?" someone shouted.

Sabine saw a young male reporter with determined brown eyes standing behind the barrier.

"Is he the one who got you out of Afghanistan?" another reporter asked.

Sabine saw a woman with short blond hair holding up a newspaper on the other side of the concrete barrier. Trying to hide her swell of foreboding, she stepped away from her parents and took the newspaper from the blonde. A security guard moved between them, but Sabine was barely aware of his protective gesture. She stared in shock at the picture on the front page of that morning's *Washington Daily,* a nationally recognized newspaper.

Big and bold, the headline read Rescued Contractor Welcomed Home.

Below that, Sabine stood in Cullen's arms, and he was kissing her like a man who'd already tasted more than her mouth. That kiss was hot and deep and full of emotion. A heartfelt goodbye. With his back to the camera, most of his face was concealed, but his lips and jaw were in clear profile. Part of one closed eye was visible through a few strands of hair. With the concrete pillar on one side and a wall on the other, there weren't many angles a camera could capture him from where he stood. Even someone who knew Cullen would have a hard time recognizing him in this photo.

Her eyes lifted. Cameras went off with a flurry.

Sabine could see the blonde around the security guard's shoulder. The woman smiled a knowing smile, then wrote furiously on her small notebook.

Sabine turned and resumed her trek to the car. Shouted questions trailed after her.

"Where is he now, Miss O'Clery? Why isn't he with you?"

"Was that a farewell kiss instead of a welcome home?"

"It's been rumored your rescue was funded by a private source. Would that be your father?"

"Is the man in that photo one of the men who got you out of Afghanistan? Does he work for your father?"

"Is it true your rescue plane crashed on a Greek island, Miss O'Clery?"

Sabine stopped in her tracks and gaped at the reporter who'd asked the last question. A tall, slender woman with dark hair and observant blue eyes stood with a ready pen. How had she learned that? Had someone recognized her in Kárpathos? Or had someone close to the mission talked?

The woman smiled. "Were you alone with your rescuer there?"

Her mother tugged her arm and she moved toward the car.

"We have no comment," Noah said. "Surely you understand my daughter needs rest."

Sabine looked back at the throng one last time. Cameras pinged and clicked.

"Get inside, baby girl."

Sabine did as her mother said. Mae followed and Noah shut the door. Tinted windows hid them from view.

Noah lowered himself into the passenger seat, and the driver, doing his best to appear unaffected by all the ruckus, maneuvered the car away from the crowd.

Noah twisted around to send Sabine an ominous look. "You left a few important details out, I see." He pointed at the copy of the *Washington Daily* in Sabine's lap. "What the hell is *that?*"

Sabine looked down at the picture, at Cullen's closed eyes, the line of his jaw and those full lips pressed to hers in a hungry kiss. She felt it all over again. The warm breath from his nose. His tongue reaching as desperately as hers. A tingle coursed through her just as it had then.

Oh, God, it was worse than she thought. How could it matter so much? They hadn't been together long enough.

"This could be damaging for him, you know. Doesn't that mean anything to you?"

"I didn't call the press, so stop blaming me." She jabbed the paper with her forefinger, venting her frustration, wishing she could turn off the emotions the photo wrung from her. "This isn't my fault!"

Beside her, her mother sucked an audible lungful of air. "So it's true?"

Feeling blood creep into her face, Sabine looked at her mother.

Mae's eyes widened. Then she looked crestfallen. "You were alone with the man Noah hired to rescue you…on a Greek island?"

"We…" Sabine faltered to hang on to her willpower and swallowed hard. Had her father only *hired* Cullen to rescue her? Who *was* he? She struggled with the hope that generated. What if he wasn't a mercenary?

Stop, she told her inner voice. He still had chosen to let her go, to never see her again.

"What happened?" her mother pressed.

In the rearview mirror, Sabine caught the driver's riveted glance.

"We…had trouble flying out of Afghanistan," she found the aplomb to say.

"The rescue helicopter was shot down, and they had to fly on low fuel to Athens," her father took over for her. "The plane crashed on Kárpathos. They were there for three days but only because Sabine wasn't well enough to travel commercially."

Sabine stared at her father. "When did Cullen tell you all that?"

Her father looked taken aback. "He *told* you his name?"

Fighting a flush with the memory of when he'd told her, Sabine stammered, "O-only his first name."

Noah cursed a line of swear words, glancing down at the photo with disgust. She couldn't tell whether it was aimed at her or Cullen.

Her mother gripped her hand and looked meaningfully into her eyes. "Did something happen between the two of you while you were on the island?"

Sabine pulled her hand away, sent her father a wary glance, saw his tightly held anger, then turned to look out the window.

"Oh, Mother Mary," Mae wailed. "Something did!"

"She's alive, damn it. Who else could have gotten her out of there?" Noah's fist pounded the dash. "I wouldn't have sent him if I hadn't known he was capable of pulling it off!"

"Are you going to see him again?" her mother asked on the heels of her father's outburst.

"No," Sabine answered shortly. Too shortly.

"Oh, baby girl…"

"The publicity will kill him," Noah said.

"She's coming home to Roaring Creek. Eventually the public interest will fade," Mae said shakily.

Noah ran his hand down his face, a clear indication of his agitation, and turned to look at Sabine. "Will you do that? Will you stay with your mother until the publicity dies down?"

Nothing appealed to her more than moving back to Roaring Creek. She belonged there. Never should have left. Maybe the woman underneath the pride-driven achievements would blossom again. All the As in physics and chemistry and calculus, all the daredevil contracting jobs, even the recognition as a distinguished hydrogeologist—none of that mattered in Roaring Creek. It was easy to agree with her father this one time.

She nodded.

"All right. Good. If anyone asks about the man in the photo, just tell them he was someone you knew from London but you ended your relationship because of your ordeal."

"I don't know if that'll wash." Mae tapped the newspaper with her finger. "Look at that. Neither one of them looks ready to give each other up."

Sabine did not want to see that picture ever again. "Don't worry, Mom. I'm never going to see him again and I'm okay with that." She looked at her father. "Trust me. I'm more than okay with that."

* * *

Cullen didn't straighten in the leather chair as Noah Page leaned over the conference room table and dropped a copy of the *Washington Daily* in front of him. It was a day old.

"What the hell is the matter with you?"

Looking at the front-page photo, reading the headline, Cullen had to cover his alarm.

"*Current Events* wants to interview my daughter on national television. What do you suppose they'll want to talk about?"

Cullen's mind raced. Where had the photographer been? It must have been a tourist or someone passing through the airport who recognized Sabine. The media couldn't have known they'd be there. Noah hadn't told a soul and neither had he. Not when someone close to the mission had leaked information about the rescue.

But how had he missed someone shooting pictures of him? Details in the photo came into sharper focus and he got his answer. Kissing Sabine had sapped his usual awareness. All he'd felt and thought while his tongue was in her mouth was how much he wished he'd spent more time with her in Kárpathos.

He raised his eyes. With his hands braced on the gleaming mahogany table, Noah's brow creased above his nose like the face of a hawk while he waited for some kind of reaction from Cullen.

Cullen hid it from him. He was too thrown by how easily Sabine had distracted him. In Kárpathos, when she'd kissed him, he'd been taken off guard by the strength of his passion. Kissing her in London had brought it all back. He couldn't, wouldn't, make the stretch and call it love, but sex with her had been equal to nothing he'd ever experienced. How was he supposed to explain that to Noah, a man who'd trusted him to save his daughter's life? A man he owed, at the very least, respect.

He looked down at the photograph again. Sabine's face had

taken the brunt of the camera's lens, but it was where their lips joined that snared his attention. He could feel what it did to him. Even now. It could be the very thing that destroyed him.

If his commander learned of his mission, there would be no way to explain himself. If his contacts in the government learned of it... He swore inside his head. They were few but went all the way up to a senator. He had to protect them all. No matter what happened to him personally.

"Has anyone recognized me?" he finally asked.

"Not that I'm aware."

Cullen let go of his held breath. Maybe he'd gotten lucky and no one had seen enough detail to make a connection. The photographer hadn't been able to get a clear shot of him. At least he'd been careful about where he chose to part ways with Sabine. Good thing he was never going to see her again. Being with her consumed him to an unnerving degree.

"It's not like you to risk your career this way," Noah said.

Cullen kept his hearty agreement to himself. To think how close he'd come to losing himself in her....

"Judging from the looks of that picture, I can hardly believe you're the same man I sent to rescue my daughter."

Hearing the leashed anger in Noah's voice, Cullen knew what really bothered him. "Nothing happened that she didn't want, Mr. Page."

Noah lifted one of his hands from the table and pointed a finger in front of Cullen's face. "Don't 'Mr. Page' me. This is my *daughter* we're talking about. I asked you to get her out of Afghanistan, not screw her on a Greek island!"

Cullen looked unflinchingly into Noah's raging eyes. "I wouldn't have touched her if I didn't think it was mutual."

"She might have been vulnerable from being held captive by terrorists," Noah said caustically. "Did you ever think of that?"

Cullen pressed his mouth tight, unable to argue. Noah's

daughter was a beautiful woman, and that beauty had muddled his brain. He wasn't accustomed to that kind of weakness.

Once Sabine started kissing him, he'd been lost in her. All thoughts of resisting had fled right along with the consequences. His career had no room for a woman like her. She needed a man who could invest the time to devote himself wholly and completely to her. He'd gleaned enough from her relationship with her father to know that much. Cullen didn't want that kind of love.

"Was she upset about never seeing you again?" Noah sounded like a worried father and made Cullen feel like a teenager in trouble for corrupting his little girl.

He faltered for words. Sabine had been upset, but not because she didn't understand the situation between them. Noah saw his hesitation, and his expression tightened with renewed rage.

"She knew I wouldn't be able to see her once we returned to the States," Cullen said quickly. But inside he wondered if she had. Before they'd made love, had she known? Even so, he doubted she'd considered the consequences until the next morning. He sure as hell hadn't.

Noah straightened and turned his back, moving to the window at one end of the conference room, where sunlight streamed through tinted glass and a view of the Miami skyline sprawled. "You shouldn't have let it happen."

Cullen lowered his gaze to the newspaper on the conference room table, studying the photograph that was sure to stir imaginations everywhere. He didn't think he could have resisted her even if he'd tried harder. The strength of it crept from nowhere and threatened to smother him.

"I'm sorry, Noah. If I hurt her, I never meant to."

Noah moved back toward the conference room table, stopping opposite from where Cullen sat.

"I owe you my life. The last thing I want to do is dishonor you or your daughter."

The rest of Noah's anger left his eyes. "You don't owe me your life. I'm more grateful to you for bringing Sabine home than you can possibly imagine."

Cullen pushed his chair back and stood, tucking his hands into the pockets of his white cotton shorts.

"What are you going to do about that?" Noah gestured to the newspaper on the table.

Knowing Noah was referring to the media, Cullen answered with his only option. "Wait until the curiosity dies down."

Noah smiled wryly. "That might take a while. Reporters are romanticizing Sabine's rescue to the hilt. It's on every channel. Everyone's wondering who the big, tall, dark-haired man is in the photo. It's you they're curious about, Cullen. More than her."

Cullen slid his hands from his pockets and lifted the newspaper to skim the article. Noah was right. In all, the article and photograph did a fine job of stirring interest in the identity of Sabine's rescuer. Sighing, he rubbed his eyes and ran his hand down his face. Kissing Sabine in the middle of an airport had to be one of the stupidest things he'd ever done.

"Well, look on the bright side," Noah said. "Even if you wanted to see her again, she wouldn't have anything to do with you anymore."

He lowered his hand. "Why not?"

"You're lower than dirt by association," Noah said, trying to sound flippant but failing.

"To you?"

"She thinks I'm a mercenary who prefers traveling the world spreading mayhem to settling down with her mother. Since I hired you to rescue her, she'll pin the same label on you."

"Mercenary."

Noah nodded.

Memories of dinner with Sabine made him chuckle.

"You find that amusing?"

"She's got fire in her, that's for sure."

Noah nodded again, looking rueful. "Got her mother's temper."

Cullen rolled the newspaper up and held it in his hand at his side. "Is that why she despises you? She thinks you're a merc?" He already knew but wanted to hear Noah's side of it.

"I was, at one time in my life. Now I just hire them."

Noah ran a private military company, but its purpose was security. Executives and foreign dignitaries hired his services, as did corporations with assets in foreign countries that needed guarding and natives who needed protection against rebel groups. For Noah, humanity came first on every mission. Sabine was wrong about him.

"You never lost sight of what was right," Cullen said.

"That's not what Sabine thinks."

"Sabine has never gotten over growing up without a father around."

"If I could have been around, I would have. I swear it."

"You don't have to convince me." Cullen smiled a little.

"She doesn't understand why I had to stay away, after years of trying to make it work with Mae."

"Why couldn't you?"

Noah turned his back, a clear attempt to hide his emotion. "I wasn't ready to give up my profession for Mae, and she wasn't willing to leave her hometown. At the time, I didn't think small-town life was for me."

"Isn't asking a man to give up his career a bit much?"

Noah faced him again. "Not if the career is controversial and keeps him from the woman he loves."

Cullen saw the genuine emotion in Noah's eyes and felt a flash of contrition. It was too close to what he'd done with Sabine—acted on concern for his career and left behind anything that might have sparked in Kárpathos. Or had it been more than that? Waking up after making love to her had knocked him off balance. The way he'd felt. He'd wanted nothing more than to get rid of her, to cut short the uneasy sensation crawling up his spine that she was like no other woman he'd met. He could fall into deep love with her. And deep love he did not do. Deep love wasn't for him. Not ever.

"It may be too late for Mae and me, but I want to make things right with my daughter," Noah said. "I want to know her and have a good relationship with her. You've given me a chance to do that, Cullen."

But not without a price. He'd lost four good men saving Sabine, and it never should have happened. No matter how many times he went over it in his head, he saw nothing he could have done differently. His plan had been solid. Nothing in the intelligence indicated they were dealing with anything other than terrorists. How could he have predicted that someone other than the kidnappers wouldn't want Sabine to make it out of there alive?

He'd have to work in the background to avoid the press, but he'd help Noah find those responsible. He wouldn't rest until he had retribution for his team.

As though reading his thoughts, Noah walked over to the center of the table and leaned over to press a button on the phone. The speaker came on and a woman answered.

"Yes, Mr. Page?"

"Bring me the al Hasan file."

"Have you found something?" Cullen asked, wondering if it would support his suspicions.

Noah didn't answer. Seconds later the conference room door opened and Noah's assistant entered the room. The slender brunette eyed Cullen up and down. Noah took the file from her.

"Thanks, Cindy."

Cindy smiled at Cullen with a smoky look. Cullen didn't encourage her. He turned his attention to Noah, and the woman left the conference room, closing the door behind her.

Noah handed him the file. He took it and put the newspaper on the table to free both hands. Opening the folder, he found a picture of Isma'il al Hasan, the leader of the group who'd kidnapped Sabine and Samuel. He flipped through other pages containing background information.

"I've confirmed he was killed in the explosion you and your team set," Noah said.

That came as good news to Cullen, for Sabine's sake. And Samuel's.

"He was a rebel who came from a wealthy family that has ties to al Qaeda," Noah went on as Cullen read. "He had the means to have a helicopter in the abandoned village where Sabine and Samuel were taken. He could have had it there all along as a precautionary measure."

Cullen shook his head. "It didn't show up in the satellite images. And that doesn't explain why someone was waiting for us in Egypt. Isma'il kidnapped your daughter, but he didn't do it for terrorism."

Noah sighed with frustration. "I've searched every angle. Why would Isma'il kidnap two American contractors for any other reason? He had confirmed ties to al Qaeda."

"Isma'il couldn't have known about the rescue mission. None of his men were expecting us. It wasn't until we were in flight with Sabine that things started to go wrong. Someone was waiting for us outside the village with the helicopter…like they didn't want Isma'il and his men to know they were there any more than we did. And mercenaries were waiting for us in Egypt like somebody hired them for the job. Whatever reason Sabine and Samuel were kidnapped, that same somebody wanted them dead."

"You think the men who attacked you knew about the kidnapping? Knew where Samuel and my daughter were being held and that Isma'il would kill them?"

Cullen said nothing, just let the plausibility of his assessment sink into Noah's mind.

"What you're suggesting is unthinkable! Who would do that? Sabine doesn't know why she was kidnapped. She couldn't tell authorities anything. She isn't a threat to anyone."

"Maybe whoever tried to stop her rescue didn't know that, or didn't want to take the chance that she did." But they must have had a reason to think she was, or might be, a threat. "Isma'il could have told them anything."

"Except he didn't."

"And now he's dead."

Noah ran his hand over his face, blowing out another long sigh.

"Sabine's kidnapping was all over the news," Cullen went on. "Her rescue is even more of a splash. What would happen if the truth got out? Who would it expose? Why did Isma'il kidnap the contractors to begin with, and why would someone want him to kill them?"

Noah stared at Cullen, his expression tight as he absorbed it all.

"Find the person who leaked the mission details, Noah. Then you'll find whoever did this." He paused. "My secretary is prepared to help in any way you need her." Odelia Frank wasn't just any secretary. The woman was amazing.

"No one in this organization would betray me like that."

"There's no other way it could have gotten out."

"The only person other than me and the operatives on your team who had access to that kind of information is Cindy, and I never told her where Sabine was, or your refueling locations."

"Could she have overheard you sometime? Maybe she or someone else stole the information without your knowledge."

"Why would she do that? Cindy is young, and she's not very bright."

Cullen didn't expect to solve everything right now. "Your daughter is in danger until you find that person, Noah. Nobody goes to that much trouble to try and kill someone if they don't have a reason to feel threatened. You can't assume it's over just because she's in the United States now." He put the file down onto the conference room table. "If I were you, I'd start with taking a harder look at Aden Archer and his company."

"Aden has been nothing but distraught over all this."

"It doesn't have to be him. It could be anyone working on that contracting job or anyone close to it."

"Sabine was there to assess groundwater conditions."

"A perfect cover for some other nefarious activity. Do you want to risk your daughter's life again?"

Without hesitation, Noah shook his head. "I'll dig deeper. I'll find who leaked the information. I just wish I had more to go on."

Gnawing dread churned inside Cullen. He was in danger of involving himself in this situation more than he could afford. This could destroy a career he'd worked years to develop. Did he want to throw it all away for a woman? No. No matter how great the urge was to go to Sabine, he had to stay away. No one could learn the truth about his company, however noble its purpose, and he had to protect the men he served. Men who could not admit to having anything to do with the creation of such a company.

"Maybe you should send someone to Roaring Creek to keep an eye on her," he said. The best he could do was make sure Sabine was safe. "The press has done a good job of convincing everyone she doesn't know why she was kidnapped, and the publicity might have scared whoever tried to kill her away for a while, but that could all change. What if Sabine gets too curious or remembers something she didn't think was significant before?"

"Don't worry. I already have someone on her. She'll be watched until we get to the bottom of this."

Wondering if the man Noah had assigned to Sabine was competent enough, wanting to ask but refusing to let himself, Cullen picked up the newspaper from the table. The photo drew him in, brought him back to the moment, and convinced him he hadn't imagined the way it felt with her. He didn't feel comfortable leaving her safety up to Noah. Or any other man, for that matter. Noah's men had experience guarding people and assets in foreign countries from rebels and other extremists. But would they know what to do with a more sophisticated foe?

He tucked the paper under his arm. "I'll have Odie call you."

Noah nodded. "I'll let you know if anything comes up."

Cullen moved toward the conference room door. The choice had been made. He'd made it when he left Sabine in London. No looking back.

Chapter 6

The media were really starting to annoy her. Sabine lifted a fondue set out of a box. In the four weeks since her return, they'd hounded her for information every chance they'd gotten. While she was no longer a headline, every now and again she'd catch a snippet about her, along with a photo. Her father's opening an office in Denver only kept the intrigue alive. He'd told the press he was doing it to be closer to his daughter. The gesture threatened to soften her defenses, something she'd done one too many times as a child—trusted her hope when she should have known better.

All she wanted to do was live a simple life here in Roaring Creek. Put Afghanistan behind her, forget her father's involvement in her rescue and his apparent change of heart. Cullen, too, though there hadn't been any sign of his leaving her mind. At least she had the bookstore to occupy her.

As soon as she'd arrived back in town, she'd seen this old

two-story building for sale and known exactly what she wanted to do. Books, and not the scientific kind, were a piece of her she'd abandoned on her way to proving her worthiness through achievements. She didn't need to keep grabbing bulls by the horns. She could open a bookstore downstairs and live a simple life above it in this two-bedroom apartment. Just the thought alone gave her a boost of elation.

"Are you sure you're ready for this? It's only been a month."

Sabine turned to see her mother put a stack of plates into the kitchen cupboard, her shoulder-length red hair up in a clip.

"I can't live with you the rest of my life, Mom."

Mae reached for a stack of bowls and put them in the cupboard, with her green eyes glancing Sabine's way. "I wouldn't mind if you did. But maybe you should have at least stayed a while longer. You know, until you were sure."

"I'm as sure as I'm going to get." Sabine put her fondue set in the cupboard above the refrigerator and stepped down from the stool. She moved to a box on the table. "You can't protect me from everything." Opening the box, she reached inside for a glass and began to unwrap it from the packing paper.

"Charlotte and Camille are close by anyway," her mother rationalized. Charlotte and Camille were twins who ran the local bakery. "If you need them, their house is just down the street."

"So are Elwin and Cloe and Buddy. I'll be all right, Mom. Like you said, there are people close by. I live in town."

"I don't like thinking of you all alone when you can't sleep."

Reminded of the dream she'd had the night before, Sabine stared at the wineglass she was about to put away. It was the same dream she'd had in Kárpathos. Details seeped into her conscience even as she tried to ward them off. The knife. Samuel. Isma'il. The face of the beast.

"Do you want to talk about it?" Mae asked.

Sabine shook her head. "It's just a bad dream."

"Maybe if you tell me about it, they won't wake you anymore."

Sabine held the wineglass tighter as the same sick feeling churned in her. In the dream, the beast turned to face her. It always started with the back of his head. There was something familiar about it. She went still.

"Sabine?" She barely heard her mother.

That was it! The beast turning…its face morphed into a man's. Someone recognizable. Sabine's heart raced.

Isma'il.

She saw him clearly for the first time. How his cold, beady eyes blazed a hateful gaze into hers. How his head turned to face Samuel, presenting the back of his head to her while he resumed the torture that had eventually killed her field partner. She couldn't go there. Couldn't remember that. It was too horrible. But another time came to her, when Isma'il walked away after one of his brutal beatings. The back of his head again.

The back of his head.

A chill spread through her skin. She'd seen it before. Her heart raced faster. No. No. It couldn't be.

"Sabine? Are you all right?" Her mother started to approach.

Too overwhelmed with the horror of her realization, Sabine didn't answer. She'd seen the back of Isma'il's head before her abduction. Aden had met him in the village where she and Samuel were working. She remembered telling Samuel about it. And he'd thought it was odd. Had he known something?

Aden had met with Isma'il.

The glass she still held slipped from her hand and shattered on the cream-colored tile floor.

Her mother gasped, watching Sabine with confused and deeply concerned eyes.

Sabine put her hand on the kitchen countertop to support herself. She was dizzy with the realization that Aden had met with the man who'd killed Samuel.

Or had he?

Was she certain Isma'il was the man Aden had met? Or were her dreams out of proportion with reality?

You couldn't tell authorities anything that might help? The question Aden had asked when she'd first arrived home in Denver echoed in her mind. Was he relieved she hadn't known why she'd been kidnapped?

"Sabine, tell me what's wrong." Her mother's voice penetrated her shock.

Sabine lifted her hand to her forehead, hearing her own breathing and feeling her rapid pulse going helter-skelter. She shook her head. "I-I'm all right." She knelt to clean up the broken glass.

Her mother knelt with her, doing a poor job of covering her sob. But Sabine couldn't summon the wherewithal to reassure her any further. She was too overwrought.

What if her dream was not so far from the truth? What if Aden had known Isma'il? Someone had gone to great lengths to try to stop her rescue. Someone other than Isma'il and his men. Had Aden wanted her and Samuel to die?

Prickles of dismay made Sabine even more sick to her stomach. Bile rose in her throat, and in the next instant she knew she was going to throw up. Rushing to the bathroom, she fell light-headed to her knees before the toilet. If Aden had known the man who'd slaughtered Samuel, had he known the reason for their abduction? Could he have prevented it?

Sabine had dry heaves above the toilet. *Samuel.* Oh, God.

Their kidnapping couldn't have had anything to do with Aden's dealings with Isma'il. It was too horrible to imagine. Yet the helicopter that had come after them, and the attack in Egypt made it plausible. Aden wouldn't want anyone to know his connection to Isma'il.

With a pale, trembling hand over her mouth, Sabine slumped

onto her rear and leaned against the wall. She still felt so ill that it made her weak. She closed her eyes and struggled to make sense of it.

"Are you pregnant?"

Sabine opened her eyes like a spring had triggered them and froze, staring up at her mother. Mae stood in the doorway of the bathroom, anxiousness tight in her brow. The consequences had mattered very little after the first time she'd kissed Cullen. She'd reached out to him after her dream, but something stronger had led to the intimacy they'd shared.

"No," she answered her mother stiffly. "It isn't that." It couldn't be, thank God. Having a baby would be the cruelest irony, following in her mother's footsteps and raising a child on her own. At least she didn't have to worry about that. At least that much about her and Cullen was different than her mother's relationship with Noah.

"Then what just happened here?"

Sabine didn't want to worry her mother if her suspicions were wrong. So she had a terrible dream… That wasn't unusual given what she'd survived. She had to be sure before she started pointing her finger at Aden.

"I was just thinking about Samuel," she said, her mind still reeling.

How could she confirm it was Isma'il whom Aden had met in the village? She'd never mentioned to the authorities that she'd seen Aden with a local villager. Nothing in the press revealed she knew anything about the reason for her abduction. She shouldn't pose a threat to anyone. But what if Samuel had known something? It would have been so like him to protect her by not telling her anything. And Aden might have assumed she knew just as much as Samuel.

Sabine drove into Denver, worrying if she was doing the right thing. She wasn't comfortable going straight to Aden. What if her dream had nothing to do with reality? It could be a by-product of her trauma. Maybe Samuel's wife could tell her something. Maybe he'd said something to her about Aden. Anything that might give Sabine a clue, confirm or dispel what the dream suggested.

She had to stop for directions at a gas station, but finally she made her way to Lisandra's house on Cathay Street, a middle-class subdivision of Aurora, Colorado. The brick-and-beige-colored tri-level had mature landscaping and a big lot. Sabine parked in the driveway, glancing around her as she walked to the front door. Ringing the doorbell, she waited. Lisandra might not even be home. Sabine hadn't called first.

But the door swung open and Lisandra stood still, staring at Sabine, obviously recognizing her from media pictures. Her thick, dark hair was up in a messy clip, and her dark eyes looked weary and lost.

"I'm sorry to stop by without calling you," Sabine said.

Lisandra opened the door wider. "Come in."

Sabine stepped inside, seeing a kitchen with hickory floors to her left, and a railing overlooking a spacious living room to her right.

"I'm sorry about Samuel," Sabine said, facing Lisandra. "He talked about you all the time."

Lisandra lowered her head. Her mouth pressed tight, as though struggling with emotion. After a moment she lifted her head again. "You didn't have to come here and tell me that."

"Actually, there's another reason I'm here." She hesitated, uncertain about how much to tell her. Not much, that's for sure. She didn't want to put the woman in any danger. "Samuel said something just before we were kidnapped. I wondered if…I wondered…well, it may be nothing but I need to be sure." She faltered for words.

"What is it? What did he say? Please, tell me."

"He seemed to think Aden's visits to the valley were odd. Did he ever say anything to you?"

"What would Aden's visits to the site have to do with your kidnapping?"

"Maybe nothing. Samuel just thought it was odd, and I wondered if he had said anything to you. Maybe in one of his letters? Even if you didn't think anything of it at the time."

Disappointment dulled Lisandra's eyes. "No. He never mentioned anything about Aden, on the phone or in any of his letters. Why? Do you think Aden knows something?"

Sabine sighed with her own disappointment. "I don't know. I may be reaching."

"No," Lisandra quickly disagreed, touching Sabine's forearm as though in emphasis. "If there's anything that will help bring Samuel's killers to justice, I'm glad to know you'll try."

Sabine nodded and didn't know what else to say.

"Envirotech did send a package to me," Lisandra said, dropping her hand.

Sabine straightened as her alertness sharpened.

"It came last week. It's his belongings from…over there." Her eyes took on a drawn look and her lower lip trembled. "I haven't been able to open it yet, but maybe you'll find something that will help you."

"Does Aden know it was sent?"

"I don't know. His name wasn't on the return address. It was from one of the other contractors."

Would Aden have checked the contents first? Maybe he never had a chance. Maybe he hadn't known the contractor had mailed it. Could she be so lucky…?

Lisandra led her past a wall and up some stairs on the other side. At the first room, she stepped aside. "There's a box in the closet."

Sabine sensed the woman's tension. Without commenting or

showing any notice, she went to the closet and started to root through the contents of the box.

Other than clothes and other personal items, she found his backpack. She lifted that out and unzipped the opening. Reaching inside, she pulled out an empty water bottle, a change of clothes, an old granola bar and finally an orange field book. Samuel's field book. He'd had it with him the day they were abducted. The contractor Lisandra mentioned must have been the one to find it and put it with Samuel's things.

She opened the front cover. Three pictures fell to the floor. She knelt and picked them up, staring with foreboding at the first. Two men she didn't recognize stood inside a narrow, badly disintegrating building with hats hanging along one side. It looked like a hat shop in a filthy bazaar somewhere. She didn't know where, only that it was somewhere in the Middle East. The second picture showed the men shaking hands. The third showed them walking toward the back of the hat shop.

Tucking the pictures back in the field book, she leafed through the pages to make sure Samuel hadn't written anything other than field notes. He hadn't.

She had no way of identifying the men in the photos, and the only person she knew who could she didn't want to see.

Sabine left Lisandra's with Samuel's field book, managing to avoid telling her about the photos. Outside, she noticed someone open the driver's door of a white minivan. A spark of apprehension sent her pulse flying. But then the man lifted a camera and started shooting pictures. In an instant, she knew that stopping for directions at the gas station had cost her this. Now Aden would know she'd come to see Lisandra. Would he wonder why?

She tried to hide the field book but feared it was already too late

"Excuse me, Ms. O'Clery!" the reporter shouted, hurrying toward her. "Whose house is this?"

Sabine reached her Jeep and climbed in.

"Did you meet your rescuer here?"

She turned a glare on the reporter and shut the Jeep door.

Revving the engine, she squealed the tires racing away. The reporter didn't try to follow. A few minutes later, she drove onto Wilcox Street in Castle Rock, just off I-25, and found the brick building her father had rented. Parking, she noticed a dark green Civic in front of the building, one she'd seen parked outside her bookstore more than once, or one like it. No, it was the same one. It had a dented front left bumper and fender and a cracked windshield. She hesitated before walking toward the darkly tinted glass windows and doors of Noah's new office.

Noah opened the door before she got there, his face tense with lines of frustration. "Where have you been?" he demanded.

She entered the building, not liking the fatherly concern she heard in his voice. The sound of remodeling under way echoed, banged and buzzed. A man with pitted skin and dark eyes leaned idly against a wall ahead of her. She tried to remember if she'd ever seen him before but couldn't.

She turned to her father. "Who is that?"

"He's supposed to keep an eye on you."

Sabine couldn't believe it. "You have someone watching me?" A *mercenary* was watching her.

"You weren't supposed to leave Roaring Creek. You said you wouldn't. He lost you on the way here. You don't know how worried I've been." Noah turned an accusatory glance on the man.

The man raised his hands in protest. "It's a long drive from Roaring Creek to Denver."

"Why didn't you tell me?" Sabine rounded on Noah.

"It's for your own good."

"My own…" She narrowed her eyes as she began to piece things together. "Why do you have someone watching me? Do you know something?"

"No, I—"

"You know something and didn't tell me." Aggravated, she growled low in her throat. "Oh, that is so like you."

"I don't know anything."

"Then why are you having me followed?"

"Where did you go?" her father demanded again, ignoring her temper.

"Tell me why you feel I need protection first."

Noah signed in resignation. "You're as stubborn as your mother." He paused before he relented. "I still don't know who tried to stop your rescue."

"But no one's come after me here in the States. Why do you think anyone would?"

"The media have done us a favor in that regard. It's obvious you don't know why you were kidnapped."

"Then I don't need a bodyguard."

"I disagree. Until I know who's behind your kidnapping, that's how it's going to be, Sabine."

She pointed her finger at him. "Don't you talk to me like that. I'm not your daughter."

"You are my daughter, and whether you like it or not, I'm going to protect you."

She narrowed her eyes at him again but held her tongue and lowered her hand.

He looked down at the field book. "What's that you're holding? Where did you go just now?"

She looked down at the book, then back up at her father. She had no choice other than to trust him with this. "I went to see Lisandra Barry. Envirotech sent her Samuel's things. I found this among them." She handed him the field book.

He took it from her and turned. She followed him into a conference room, glancing at the man with pitted skin on her way. He stayed behind, a silent watcher. Her bodyguard. It frightened her to know her father thought she needed one.

Inside the conference room, Noah closed the door and faced her. He opened the cover and found the photos, taking his time looking at each one. At last, he raised his head.

"Do you know who these men are?"

She shook her head. "That's why I came here." The only reason.

He looked down at the top photo in his hand. "I've been to this bazaar before."

"In the photo?" Then she realized. Of course, in his active days as a mercenary, he'd been there.

"It's the Khyber Bazaar, not far from the Afghanistan border in Pakistan."

"What does it mean?"

"I don't know. Maybe nothing. But as soon as I know something, I'll tell you. I promise."

He was going to tell her? Noah? She was taken aback. And she believed him, which made her uneasy. It sneaked past her defenses and warmed her.

"You told me you'd stay in Roaring Creek," he said, repeating his earlier comment.

"I…"

"I need you to stay there, Sabine. No more driving alone down the mountain and into the city where anything can happen to you."

He seemed genuinely concerned. She wanted to tell him about her dream, but she stopped herself. It was too easy to fall into old patterns and trust him with her heart. The dream disturbed her too much. She wasn't comfortable with him seeing that much of her emotions.

"What do you know about Aden?" she asked instead.

"Archer? Why are you asking?"

"He might know something about the kidnapping. Samuel and I were his contractors."

He studied her face and she could see his question. Why was she asking? She appreciated that he didn't press her. "So far, he's clean. Don't go near him, Sabine. You leave that to us. You stay in Roaring Creek, do you understand?"

"Us?"

He hesitated. "Me and the others working to find the people who tried to stop your rescue."

Cullen? Was he still involved? She didn't welcome the surge of warmth that thought gave her. She decided not to ask her father. The last thing she needed was to start wondering if Cullen cared more than she thought.

"I don't want you digging any deeper into this, Sabine. If Aden was involved in your kidnapping, I don't want him to have a reason to get nervous."

She looked down at the field book. It might be too late for that. But she nodded to her father.

Late the next afternoon, Sabine was about to leave for the supermarket when a buzzer sounded, indicating that someone was at her back door. Going down the stairs and into the office behind what would soon be her bookstore, she peered through the peephole and saw Aden.

The shock of it gave her a jolt. What was he doing here? It was too much of a coincidence after the blurb of her visit to Samuel's wife. But if she didn't answer the door, she might lose an opportunity to learn something. Besides, her father had found nothing incriminating against him. And she had her very own mercenary for a bodyguard.

Too curious not to, she opened the door.

Aden smiled without showing any teeth, his narrow face framed by thin, straight, dark hair. "Sabine."

"Hello, Aden."

"I came by to see how you were doing. I hope you don't mind."

She shook her head. Instead of letting him inside, she stepped out onto the back stairs and left the door open. "I'm fine. You could have just called instead of driving all this way."

"I had to see for myself." His brown gaze took a quick look over her before meeting her eyes again. "You look great."

"Thank you," she said. Was he telling the truth, or did he have another reason for coming here?

"Things seem to keep popping up in the news about you," he commented.

"Everyone loves a happy ending." She smiled cheekily, while inside her heart flew. Why was he bringing that up?

"Was it a happy ending for you?"

"I'm alive."

"No, I mean about that man in the *Washington Daily* photo."

She knew what he meant. "Oh." She didn't know what else to say.

"They keep waiting to catch you with him," he said.

"I suppose the London airport photo is to blame for that."

"No supposing about it." Aden grinned.

In other words, the photo revealed an intriguing amount of passion between her and her mysterious rescuer. She hid her discomfort. She could still feel that kiss whenever she saw that picture.

"Did you meet him at Lisandra Barry's like the article speculates?"

She breathed a single laugh to cover her anxiety. He was leading up to something. "No."

"Why did you go there, then?"

"I haven't seen Lisandra since I came home. I wanted to pay my respects."

Was that doubt she saw cross his eyes? "The photo showed you holding a field book," he said. "Was it Samuel's?"

She hesitated. "You noticed I was holding his field book?"

"Why did you take it with you?"

"Why do you want to know?"

His smile was too wily. "Someone tried to stop your rescue. I'm as interested as your father in finding out why."

She didn't believe him. "You talked to my father?"

"He came to ask me some questions."

"Really?" She tried to sound surprised. "Why did he question you?"

"Do you have the field book?" he asked instead of answering.

Cold apprehension rushed her. Did he know about the photos? How? He must not have been able to find them before they were shipped to Lisandra, and now he suspected they were hidden in the field book.

"You're awfully persistent over something as benign as a field book," she hedged.

He didn't say anything, just looked at her with steady, unflinching eyes.

They were playing cat and mouse, and she had to let him know she wasn't planning on being the mouse. "I saw you meet with one of the locals in the village where we were working," she said, hoping it wasn't a mistake. "Maybe that has more to do with why you're here than Samuel's field book."

He stared at her for several more seconds. "Who did you see me meet?"

"I was going to ask you that very same thing, Aden."

His eyes narrowed. "Be careful, Sabine. This goes deeper than just me."

Chills sprinkled down her arms. Her pulse quickened. He may as well have admitted his involvement outright.

"Aden, if you know something…"

A sound to her left made her turn with him. The man from

the dark green Civic emerged from around the corner of her building, walking with a slow, long stride, watching Aden.

"Is everything all right here?" he asked.

"Fine," she said, eyeing Aden.

"I was just leaving," he said, meeting her look. "If I could have done something to help you over there, I would have, Sabine. Remember that."

What did he mean? Was he trying to tell her he was a victim like her?

Or had he met with Isma'il and played a hand in her and Samuel's kidnapping, one he now wished he could withdraw?

The next morning, Sabine parked in the grocery store lot. As she locked her car, her mind still raced with everything Aden had said, and what he hadn't. Her bodyguard had questioned her about Aden's visit and said he'd relay the information to Noah. She hadn't told him about her dream, though. What would it gain? Noah had already questioned Aden, and Aden wasn't talking.

"Ms. O'Clery?"

Turning, Sabine saw a tall, slender woman with short dark hair approach from the direction she'd just come.

"Rhea Graham with *Current Events.*"

A sinking feeling tumbled through her middle. She didn't move to take the woman's outreached hand.

"We've been trying to reach you by phone," Rhea said. "I'm sorry to sneak up on you like this, but you really gave us no other alternative."

Facing the reporter fully, Sabine cocked her head at the woman's audacity.

"Have you given some more thought to doing an interview with us?" Rhea asked.

"I don't need to. I'm not doing an interview. Not with anyone.

I'm sorry, you've wasted your time coming here." She started toward the grocery store entrance.

The reporter kept up with her. "How important is it to you to keep your rescuer's identity a secret, Ms. O'Clery?"

Sabine's steps slowed and she glanced at the woman.

"Someone close to your father knew things about your rescue no one else could," Rhea said. "It's how we learned of your crash-landing in Greece. With a little more digging, it won't be long before we have a name."

Sabine stopped altogether and faced the woman again. How much had her contact told her? It couldn't have been too much, or it would have been all over the news by now. "My father isn't that careless in his line of work."

"Are you sure about that? I thought you were estranged from him."

True. She had no way of knowing whom her father employed, much less about those he'd entrusted with information concerning her rescue. But even if he'd made a mistake, Cullen wouldn't have. "You're bluffing."

"Are you willing to take that chance?" In Sabine's silence, she added, "This contact says she has a phone number. We're working on convincing her to give it to us. She claims the number can be traced to the man your father hired to rescue you."

"Her?"

The reporter smiled. "It's your story we want, Ms. O'Clery. The more people who are curious about your rescuer, the more our ratings go up. The man in the *Washington Daily* photo can stay a mystery as long as the public stays interested…as long as you want him to stay a mystery."

"You can't trace his number. He wouldn't have used a traceable line." Cullen wasn't a stupid man. Then again, there was a picture of him kissing her in the London airport.

The reporter smiled. "Maybe not. But if we keep looking,

eventually something will turn up. A tiny clue that leads to a slightly bigger one that leads to something else." She raised her brow with a sly look. "He can't hide forever."

Sabine felt her pulse throb and tried to conceal her growing need for more air. "You're saying that if I agree to this interview, you won't try to expose the man who saved my life."

"That's exactly what I'm saying. But only if he stays away from you. If we see him with you, the deal is off."

"You won't." If she'd learned anything from her father, it was that a man like Cullen would have no problem staying away.

"Then you'll do it?"

"How do I know you'll keep your word? And what about other reporters?"

"No one other than me knows about the contact who's close to your father."

"Tell me who she is."

"Do you agree to do the interview?"

"I'll talk about the rescue, but I refuse to talk in detail about my captivity. Or the men who rescued me."

"Agreed."

"Now tell me the name of your contact."

Chapter 7

"Isn't your girlfriend going to be on *Current Events* this morning?"

Cullen sent Penny a withering glance from the kitchen, where he was helping Luc pack for yet another fishing trip. Both of them had been making comments like that ever since he'd arrived to wait out the Sabine O'Clery media frenzy. "She's not my girlfriend." And she better not have agreed to appear on national television.

From the chair at the end of the table, his uncle's eyes lifted from his tackle box and Cullen could read his silent skepticism.

Something had happened between him and Sabine in Kárpathos and his uncle knew it. It didn't help that his uncle had seen the newspaper he'd taken from Noah's conference room. Cullen had taken it on impulse. He'd been surprised by how much the photo revealed. More than a kiss between a man and a woman, it showed how invested they were in each other. How invested he'd been. Maybe still was.

The television went from a commercial to the *Current Events* show. A blond anchorwoman started talking.

"A little more than a month ago, Sabine O'Clery was rescued from her captors by a group of men working independently from the U.S. government…."

Cullen rose to his feet as the anchorwoman continued. What the hell was she doing? He raged inside. Why had she agreed to appear on *Current Events*? She was going to ruin him yet!

"She and one other contractor were assessing groundwater conditions in the Panjshir Valley when they were abducted and taken to an abandoned village. Little is known about the group who captured the contractors, but their leader, a man by the name of Isma'il al Hasan, is believed to have ties to al Qaeda. One of the contractors was killed during captivity, but Sabine O'Clery was miraculously spared." The short-haired, midthirties anchorwoman turned to Sabine. "Ms. O'Clery, can you tell us what happened the day you were captured?"

The camera moved to Sabine. In a black pantsuit with a white blouse under a stylish jacket, she glowed with health. Cullen couldn't help noticing other things, too. Though she sat on a sofa and her clothes covered her well, he could tell she'd gained weight. Her face was fuller, her curly red hair shinier. She was even more striking than he remembered. Her green eyes stood out with the dark lines of her lashes, and her lips were glossy and full of color.

Cullen realized he'd tuned out what she was saying as the anchorwoman asked her about her job and what she was doing in Afghanistan. He was that absorbed in seeing her again. The sight of her fed his starved eyes. He didn't know what to do with such a foreign inundation of feeling. She threw him off center. And a gnawing desire mushroomed in him to find her, be with her again.

"What happened to the other contractor? Why were you the one who survived?"

Cullen watched her face as the question was asked, saw how her eyes grew blank with memory. Why had she agreed to this interview? She must have had a reason. Was she doing it to spite her father? Him? To gain popularity? Money? What?

"I—I don't know why…." He saw her swallow. Her eyes lowered.

"It must have been terrible."

Sabine didn't respond to what Cullen thought was a lame attempt to get her to talk. After a few seconds the anchorwoman gave up and tried a new approach.

"Did you see what happened to the other contractor?" Cullen tensed with the question.

"I'm sorry, I can't talk about it. I just can't." She shook her head and he knew she was struggling with her emotions. Her hands were gripped tightly in lap.

"Was he tortured?"

Sabine moved her eyes to look at the anchorwoman. The slight quiver of her hair told Cullen she was starting to tremble. He wanted to reach through the television and choke the anchorwoman for asking such a difficult question. Obviously, she had seen what happened to the other contractor, and it had been horrific.

Sabine turned from the anchorwoman and looked into the camera that was focused on her. For an instant Cullen felt as though she were looking right at him, and it arrowed straight into his heart.

"Can you tell us what happened to Samuel? Samuel Barry."

A photo of Samuel smiling with his wife appeared on the screen.

Tears visibly pooled in Sabine's eyes. Cullen's hand curled into a fist, and he realized he'd moved closer to the television, oblivious to Penny and Luc.

"I'm sorry," the anchorwoman said. "I know this must be hard for you."

He watched Sabine fight for control of her crumbling emotions. "I can't…talk about that. You agreed not to…" A tear slid down her cheek.

"I understand. How about you tell us what happened when you were rescued, then?"

Sabine took the tissue the anchorwoman extended to her. Her eyes had that haunted, faraway look of someone who'd seen horrors no one else could imagine. Or ever wanted to.

"Who was it that organized the mission?" the anchorwoman asked.

Sabine stared at some point in the studio and answered absently, "I don't know."

"If it wasn't the U.S. military, then who was it?"

Sabine's head turned slowly toward the anchorwoman. "I wouldn't know anything about how my rescue was planned."

"Your father owns a company called Executive Indemnity Corporation, with headquarters in Miami. There have been reports on some of their activities. Your father's company is a private military company, isn't that right?"

Sabine didn't comment.

"Was it your father who organized your rescue?" the anchorwoman asked.

"My father abandoned me before I was born."

"So you're saying it wasn't your father who organized your rescue?"

"No, I'm saying my father hasn't been a part of my life. Ever."

"But he must care about you or he wouldn't have helped to free you from your captors."

Sabine said nothing, but Cullen could see she was torn, as though she wanted her father to care about her but didn't want to believe or couldn't bring herself to believe he did. Even though he'd arranged her rescue.

"Did your father hire the man in the *Washington Daily* photo? Does he know the man shown in that picture?"

"I don't know who rescued me." A true enough statement, Cullen thought with a pang of regret.

The anchorwoman smiled too shrewdly for his comfort. "What happened that day, Sabine? How were you rescued?"

Sabine sighed and cleared her throat, sitting rigidly in the chair. "A soldier broke down the door and told me he was from the United States and that he was going to get me out of there."

"A soldier? So he's U.S. military?"

"That's what I thought. I—I mean, that's what I assumed. He never said who he was."

"Is he the man in the photo from the *Washington Daily*?"

The stirrings of anger appeared in Sabine's eyes. "The man who rescued me was part of a team of several other men. I was flown to an airstrip, where a plane was waiting to fly me to London."

A very brief explanation of what had actually occurred. Cullen was impressed. She'd also avoided answering the woman's question.

"Your helicopter crashed before you made it out of Afghanistan, isn't that correct?"

Sabine wondered if that piece of information had gotten out along with the plane crash.

"Yes, but another one arrived shortly after and took us to an airstrip."

"Where was the airstrip?"

"I don't know. I wasn't aware of much except the fact that I was getting out of Afghanistan."

"What happened once you were on the plane?"

"I was flown to London."

"Didn't the plane crash?"

Sabine didn't answer the anchorwoman. He could see she knew as well as he where this line of questioning was going.

Hadn't she considered this possibility when she'd agreed to appear on national television?

"We have it from a reliable source that your plane crashed on a Greek island."

Sabine's anger fired hotter in her eyes. She pinned the anchorwoman with a warning stare. "One of the men on the team was forced to crash-land the plane. We didn't know where we were at the time. We knew we were on an island somewhere in the Mediterranean, but it wasn't until we walked to a nearby village that we knew it was Kárpathos."

Cullen cringed at her use of the word *we* after referring to "one of the men."

"When you say, 'we,' do you mean you and the man in the *Washington Daily* photo?"

Sabine blinked twice but didn't lose her cool. "No," she lied.

"Why did both the helicopter and the plane crash?"

"The plane didn't really crash. It was more of a rough landing."

"But what caused both the helicopter and the plane to go down?"

"The helicopter was shot down during the rescue."

"And the plane?"

"I'm not sure, exactly."

"Do you think it's possible terrorists held you captive and tried to kill you when you escaped?"

"Yes, that's possible."

"Could it have been anyone else?"

A brief pause. "I don't see how." Cullen saw the doubt in her eyes and wondered if anyone else could. Her vague answers were enough to raise curiosity.

"It's ironic that you were forced to land where you did. What was it like to find yourself in the middle of paradise after surviving such a terrible ordeal?"

Cullen felt like cursing loudly.

"We were very lucky to make it to an island. We could have crashed into the sea."

"Very lucky, indeed." The anchorwoman nodded, her accompanying smile knowing. She let a second or two pass. "We spoke with one of the villagers in Kárpathos, where the destroyed plane was discovered." Cullen inwardly grimaced, knowing his predicament was about to get much, much worse. "A woman who recognized you from this photograph," she held the cover of *Washington Daily* up into the camera's view, "told us she saw a man carry you through the village to a local pension. She described you as newlyweds whose private plane had crashed on the island. She said you were alone with this man and didn't leave your hotel room for two full days, and when you did finally leave it, the two of you walked down to a secluded beach, where you spent more time alone together. She invited you to her taverna, which she said you accepted and shared a romantic dinner. Octopus, I believe, is what she said you both ate that night."

Sabine's green eyes were wide with shock, and her face flushed a telling shade of red. She stared at the anchorwoman with her lips slightly parted, no doubt to accommodate for the rapid breaths he could see she was taking. She might as well admit defeat now. Every inch of her body communicated without words that everything the anchorwoman said was true. Damn her. Didn't she know the media would focus on all the speculation surrounding the plane crash?

Cullen closed his eyes and pinched the bridge of his nose, wanting to groan.

There was a poignant silence on the television, and he was certain millions of Americans were riveted by this new turn of events.

"Was the man you were with one of your rescuers? The man in the *Washington Daily* photo?"

Cullen looked over his fingers at the television and Sabine's flushed face.

"I can't…comment on that."

The anchorwoman smiled. "Did you have an affair with him?"

"I'm sorry, I—"

"Are you still?"

"No!"

Cullen ran his hand down his face with a rough sigh. She was killing him.

His uncle grunted a derisive laugh. "You might as well kiss that company of yours goodbye, son."

Sabine parted a section of the wooden blinds on her living room window and saw the white minivan still parked down the street. It was after ten p.m. The throng of reporters that had swarmed her bookstore after her appearance on *Current Events* had dwindled to this single man. Minivan Man, she was going to start calling him. He was an annoying, persistent little fellow, waiting like a dog frothing at the mouth for a chance to catch her with her secret lover.

Disgusted, she let the blinds go and carried her glass of iced tea toward the stairs. After the *Current Events* broadcast, the news had buzzed with curiosity over Cullen's identity and romanticized what had mushroomed into their torrid affair on a Greek island. The hype disturbed her, mostly because it made her think about Kárpathos—and Cullen—too much.

She stepped down the narrow stairway and emerged into the bookstore office. Flipping on lights as she went, she entered the main area of the bookstore. She passed a section of tall empty shelves where boxes of books were scattered and put her glass of iced tea on the checkout counter near the front of the store.

The books she'd ordered had arrived earlier that day but she'd waited for the cover of night to begin unpacking them. She'd dipped into her 401(k) to buy a collection of general fiction, literary fiction, nonfiction, children's books and touristy books about the region to stock her shelves. The front corner of the bookstore was under renovation and would be a coffee counter with a few quaint round tables near the front windows. Maybe she'd plant flowers in pots on the sidewalk in front of the building this summer.

A noise in the back of the store made her go still. Holding three hardcover books in her hand, she looked toward her office. Rows of shelves formed a hallway that was slightly offset from the office entrance, so she couldn't see it from where she was. Was someone in there?

Her heart started to beat faster. She put the books down and stood. Moving to the checkout counter, she pulled out the 9mm pistol she kept on the shelf under the register. Buddy from the liquor store had taught her how to use it after she'd come home from Afghanistan. Inserting a loaded clip, she moved out from behind the counter and headed for her office, holding the pistol with both hands and pointing it ahead of her. The hallway of shelves allowed her to keep out of view of the doorway leading to the office.

The sound of the back door opening made her jump into the space between the last two shelves near her office door. She closed her eyes and willed herself to have courage. Someone had broken into her bookstore. Blood drained from her head and she fought the rise of an all-too-familiar fear.

Footsteps shuffled. It sounded like more than one person. One grunt accompanied another. She leaned around the corner of the shelf. Two men crossed the doorway, locked in a fighting struggle. Both held a gun and both gripped the other's arm to prevent either from taking aim. She recognized her bodyguard, the smaller of the two. The bigger man tripped him and he fell.

She had to do something. Gun raised, she emerged from the row of shelves and hurried to the office door. Peering around the frame, she saw the bigger man standing over her bodyguard, aiming his weapon. A file cabinet blocked most of his body from her. He was going to shoot the man on the floor.

"No!" Sabine shouted and fired her pistol.

But the big man fired, too, one silenced shot that hit her bodyguard. She could tell because he groaned and rolled onto his side. She saw only his chest and head, but it was enough to know he struggled to reach his gun, which was too far away.

Sabine didn't have time to help him. The big man—tall, lean, with dark hair and eyes—swung his weapon toward her. She pivoted and ran from the office, ducking behind the first row of empty shelves, hearing a bullet hit wood. She fired her gun through the space of a shelf, forcing the man to stay behind the wall of the office. Her gun wasn't muffled and the explosions rang her ears. She ran to the end of the row and moved up the next one, crouching low, trying to see through the mesh of shelving.

Hearing the sound of slow footfalls on her wood floor, fear cauterized her. That awful fear. She moved along the shelf. The man appeared around the edge of the row. She fired again. He jumped behind the shelf. She turned to run, heard him chase her. Before she made it to the end of the row, he tripped her from behind. She went down on her hands and knees, the gun skittering from her grasp and bouncing off the wall just ahead of her. Rolling to her rear, she kicked her leg up and connected with the big man's hand. His gun went sailing over the top of the shelf to her left and fell to the floor on the other side.

The man unbuckled his belt and whipped it free of his black jeans. Sabine rolled back onto her hands and knees and scrambled toward her gun. She would not fall prey to anyone ever again. She'd kill this man without a second thought!

The tether of her hair stopped her. The man yanked her back toward him. Her scalp stung where he pulled. He looped the belt around her neck and released her hair. Sabine clawed at the belt as it tightened on her throat, furious with herself for allowing this to happen.

Choking for air, and getting little, she reached for something, anything that would provide her a weapon. Her pistol still lay a few feet away, too far for her to reach. A box she'd opened but hadn't begun to empty yet was right next to her. She reached inside for a hardback Webster's dictionary and aimed the corner at her assailant's head. With a hard wallop, she hit something that made him grunt and loosen his hold. She yanked the belt from her throat, gagging and gasping as she crawled for her gun. She stretched her arm. Her fingers curled around the handle. Rolling onto her back, she started firing.

The man scrambled to escape the explosion of bullets. She emptied her gun.

He ran into her office. She followed but only when she heard her bodyguard fire his gun. A shout and the big man's stumble told her he was hit, but he managed to run out the back door before her bodyguard could finish him off.

Reclining on a hammock in his uncle's backyard, Cullen rested his head on one folded arm, his other hand on his stomach. He chewed on a straw left over from the chocolate milk Penny had given him while he occupied himself watching white puffy clouds pass over the branches of a cottonwood tree. All this peace and quiet gave him entirely too much time to think. And all he thought about was Sabine.

Maybe he should take a trip somewhere. An exotic beach resort or something similar. The only thing stopping him was his fear that he'd be recognized. He could just go home, too, but what was there that wasn't here? A big city, for one, and he didn't think that was a good place to lay low. A suburb of Washington, D.C., was nothing like the wide open spaces of Montana.

On the patio, Luc sat on his lawn chair watching a fishing show. Cullen liked fishing but enough was enough. Once a year was enough. Every day was nauseating.

As though hearing his thoughts, Luc turned the channel. Cullen felt bad for thinking bad of his uncle's favorite pastime. Luc was getting older and couldn't keep up the pace he'd once kept in the military.

Luc stopped surfing at a news program.

"Authorities are speculating whether the man who attacked O'Clery in her Roaring Creek bookstore was responding to her recent interview on *Current Events*."

Cullen lifted his head, instantly focused on the television. His stomach muscles tightened as he rose halfway between sitting and reclining. A picture of Sabine disappeared from the screen, and the news program went to commercial.

Cullen swung his feet over the hammock and stood, shards of fear shooting through him. "What happened?" He stepped onto the patio, where his uncle had a television mounted below the eave of his house. "What happened to her?" He knew he sounded frantic. He felt frantic. And he was not accustomed to that.

Luc glanced up at him, then quickly surfed until he found another news channel. A video of Sabine being helped out of a storefront ripped through him. That haunted look was back in her eyes. She held a hand to her throat, but it didn't hide the red and chafed skin there. Something dark and uncontrollable expanded in him. He tried to steady his breathing.

"Sabine O'Clery, the woman rescued more than a month ago from Afghanistan, narrowly escaped with her life late last night after two men broke into her Roaring Creek bookstore. One man, who reportedly tried to help her, was shot and taken to a nearby hospital. Doctors say he'll recover, and guards posted at his room are refusing to let anyone but police question him. O'Clery said she and the injured man fired at her assailant, but he managed to get away. Local authorities are searching for the suspect and aren't releasing the identity of the man hospitalized during the attack."

The screen showed a picture of Noah in one corner. "Noah Page, O'Clery's estranged father, is founder and CEO of the private military company rumored to have arranged her rescue from Afghanistan, where she was held prisoner for more than two weeks. Page denies any ties to the man hospitalized during the latest attempt on her life. Roaring Creek authorities aren't commenting whether the attempt on O'Clery's life is related to her kidnapping in Afghanistan…."

Cullen let go of a vicious curse.

"Some quack tried to off her?" Luc asked, incredulous.

Someone had nearly succeeded in killing Sabine. Noah had told him about her visit to Samuel's wife and the photos she'd found. He'd worried about Aden showing up at her bookstore, too. Now there was no doubt; Aden knew about the photos. But was Sabine's finding them enough reason to kill her? He and Noah were missing something. What did Aden have to hide, and who were the men in those photos?

Cullen stormed through the house and went to the guest room, where he found his cell phone. Punching numbers with trembling fingers, he waited until Noah answered.

"What happened?" he said flatly.

"Cullen?"

"Someone tried to kill Sabine."

"I know. I've been trying to reach you but your phone was off. Cullen—"

He couldn't get a grip on the feelings swarming him. It was such a foreign sensation. "What have you learned about the chopper that fired at us? Has Odie been in touch with you?"

"Your resources are helping, Cullen. It's just going to take some time."

Cullen dug his fingers through his hair and stopped trying to hide his unease. He swore and it came from the depths of his soul. He was sick with worry.

"Don't do anything rash," Noah warned.

Cullen pinched the bridge of his nose, fighting a too-powerful urge to go to Sabine. To see for himself that she was all right and to keep her that way. All the years he'd worked to get where he was, and he was willing to throw it all away for a woman? He didn't understand what was happening to him.

"I'll send more men," Noah said. "I'll send twenty if I have to. Cullen, you aren't responsible for this. *Stay away from her.*"

Cullen moved across the guest room and didn't reply for several seconds. When he spoke, he feared it was from his heart and nothing else.

"Don't send anyone, do you understand? I'll be there by tomorrow night."

He disconnected the call and stood staring out the window of the guest room. What was he *thinking?* If the media was thick around Sabine before, they'd be like ticks on a dog's ass by now.

He paced the room. Ran his fingers through his hair once again. Sighed hard. Going to Sabine right now was suicide for his career, both with the reserves and his company.

He leaned with his hands against the wall beside the window and shut his eyes, breathing faster than normal. How could he ignore the attempt on her life? How could he go on as though he'd never gone to Afghanistan to free her? As though he'd never made love to her? He couldn't, that's how.

No matter what it cost him in the end, no matter how he felt about this unreasonable drive to risk everything for her, he couldn't stand by and watch the news to find out what happened next.

He had to do something.

* * *

Three days after her attack, Sabine folded a towel and stacked it with the rest on the kitchen table. It was late for doing laundry, but she'd had the dream again and had given up on getting any more sleep for the night.

What sounded like floorboards creaking downstairs made her go still. She listened for a while. The washer had finished its cycle but she hadn't loaded the drier yet, so the apartment was quiet. Another creak sent her pulse leaping. Someone was in her bookstore. *Again.*

Turning, she lifted the handset of the telephone in her kitchen. No dial tone. Her breathing quickened and she fought that too-familiar fear. Yesterday, she'd practiced for several hours with Buddy, shooting her pistol. If the man who'd attacked her had returned, this time she wouldn't miss.

Putting the phone down, she went to her bedroom for the gun, stepping lightly. She slid in a clip and made sure the gun was ready to fire. With a deep breath to bolster her nerve, she left her room and moved carefully to the door leading to the lower level. The hardwood floor was cold on her feet. Pausing at the door, she heard only silence on the lower level, which only made her more nervous. Silence could be more terrifying than any sound. She didn't like the memory of that.

Turning off the kitchen light, she slowly turned the doorknob. Opening the door a crack, she looked down the narrow stairs. No one was there. She opened the door a fraction wider, not making a sound, aiming the pistol down the stairs.

Assured she was alone and out of sight for now, Sabine stepped down the stairs on tiptoe, avoiding the areas she knew would creak. At the bottom, she stopped to listen. No sound. Not one.

Around the wall, in the moonlight, she spotted a man standing near the back door of her bookstore. He was dressed all in black, and it frightened her to see he also wore a black mask over his head. He was taller than the man who'd attacked her. Bigger, too. At the moment he was pointing a big gun with a silencer through a narrow opening of the door, his back to her as he appeared to be watching for something outside.

She stepped softly toward him. Holding her pistol with both hands, she stopped and aimed for his head. At this distance, she wouldn't miss if she fired.

He seemed to sense her presence then. His head turned slightly and he went very still.

"Don't shoot," he said without looking at her.

His voice flustered her. There was something familiar about it. He raised his hands and slowly turned.

All she saw of him beneath his cover of black was the glitter of his eyes. They were light in color but she couldn't tell what shade. He was very tall. As tall as…

"Drop the gun," she said, without finishing the thought, afraid it would distract her too much.

He didn't move, which gave her time to notice more about him. His tactical canvas pants with cargo pockets fit close to his hips and legs without being tight. His shirt was made of the same durable material but molded to his muscular upper body and still managed to appear flexible.

She adjusted the aim of her gun. "Drop it. Now. Or I'll pull this trigger."

She watched him blink before he slowly lowered the gun to the floor, bending, then straightening.

"Don't shoot," he said again, standing with his hands spread wide so she could see they were empty.

That voice…

He took a step toward her, sending her heart skittering. "Don't move!" A tremble shook her hands.

"Sabine—"

That rasp…she knew that voice.

He knew her name.

While she struggled with what this information meant, he sprang into action. He moved so fast she didn't see what he'd actually done until she felt a sting on her wrists and her pistol went flying. The same instant she realized she was no longer armed, she felt her feet swept out from under her and found herself on her butt. Dazed, she watched as the man crouched for his weapon smooth as a cat.

"Stay here," he said, then ran out the door.

"What—" Sabine gave herself a mental shake and jumped to her feet.

Grabbing her pistol, she ran through the door after him. She stopped and looked left and right, seeing nothing through the darkness. A sound brought her head whipping back to her left. She ran with her gun pointed to the ground, holding it with both hands. She ignored her cold feet and bare arms as she reached the corner of the building. Leaning forward, she peered around the corner. There was only a field to the west of her bookstore, which was located on the west edge of town, but a street light to the south illuminated the man dressed in black chasing another figure into the street.

Sabine ran after them. What was happening? Why were two men sneaking around her bookstore in the middle of the night— *again?*

She watched the man in black catch the second figure, a lean man who was not as tall. Tripped by quick and agile feet, the shorter man fell in the street. Before he could regain his balance, the man in black struck him with his gun. The shorter man went limp.

Was he dead?

The man in black hefted the shorter man up and over his shoulder then turned to look back. Sabine felt goose bumps from more than cold raise the flesh on her arms. But instead of coming toward her, he walked the opposite direction across the street.

He might as well have been carrying a sack of grain for all the trouble it took him to step up the curb and open the front door of the vacant building across the street…directly across from her bookstore and apartment. He left the front door open as he disappeared inside, as though beckoning her to follow.

Wary of the familiarity she felt toward him, she did. Somewhere in the depths of her mind she knew who he was. But the implications of his being here, in Roaring Creek, with an unconscious man in a vacant building, were too much for her to accept all at once.

Shivering from cold and apprehension, she put her hand against the door frame and tried to see through the darkness inside the building. A light snapped on, illuminating a stairway leading to a lower level, a basement.

She didn't want to go down there, but curiosity moved her feet for her. She paused halfway when she heard the clatter of something metal. Taking several deep breaths, she stepped the rest of the way down the stairs.

The basement was small. A single bulb lit the open space, deep shadows swallowing the far wall. A modern furnace looked out of place surrounded by the old wood and stone frame of the house. The man in black stood with his arms at his side, pistol hanging from his right hand. Sabine felt him looking at her through the twin holes of his mask.

Next to him, the figure from the street was on his knees, and his hands were tied by a chain that slung him from a pipe running across the ceiling, the metal clatter she'd heard. It was the man who'd attacked her in her bookstore. She stared at the man in black. How had he known? A riot of emotions warred in her, resistance against what a deeper part of her already knew.

Sliding his pistol into the waist of his black pants, the man in black moved toward her. His head barely fit under the low ceiling. His power lurked in the play of sinewy muscles beneath his dark covering, in the sheer size of him, long thighs, big shoulders and arms. She would have taken an instinctive step back if she hadn't been so frozen with disbelief.

The closer he came, the clearer she saw his eyes. When he stopped before her, she could no longer cling to doubt. Those eyes had looked into hers with naked, intimate heat.

When he reached to pull off the mask, she stopped breathing. Black hair fell in disarray around his head, and the full impact of his gray eyes was just as intense as she remembered, but tinged with a familiar energy. Focused and ready for combat. His gaze lowered down the front of her, unhurried, remembering, as she was. Dressed only in her thin white cotton top and matching pajama pants, she felt stripped by that look.

"Cullen," she whispered.

He lifted one gloved hand and traced the bruise on her neck. The trail of his finger left a tingle on her skin. She stood still while he told her without words what had drawn him here. His gaze shifted and met hers, burning hotter with the promise of vengeance.

She stepped back, out of his reach, not at all trusting herself with the way he made her feel. Her gaze passed over the man secured by the chain and then around the dark basement.

"We have to call the sheriff." She started to turn.

Cullen took hold of her arm just above her elbow and pulled her back to face him. "No sheriff."

She curled her hand over his biceps, meaning to push him away. Instead fiery awareness of the iron-hard muscle shot through her.

"That's the second time that man tried to attack me," she spat. "We have to report it."

"No police. No reporters. I don't want anyone knowing I'm here."

"Then why did you come? I don't need your help anymore."

His eyes indicated the bruises on her neck. "Go home, Sabine. You don't have to worry about anyone hurting you again. I'll make sure you're safe from now on."

"Go *home?*" She tugged her arm and he let her go. "And what? Forget you're here? That you have a man tied by a *chain* in the basement of what I thought was a *vacant building* that happens to be *right across the street from my bookstore?*" She couldn't help looking at Cullen's body again, so huge and ominous dressed in black. Disturbed by the warming reaction the sight gave her, she turned and climbed the stairs.

On the first level, she stood in the middle of the empty room, uncertain what to do. The house didn't appear lived-in. Something caught her eye. Near the window sill on an upside-down cardboard box, silhouetted by the streetlight, was a pair of binoculars. She went there, staring at the binoculars a moment before looking out the window. Her bookstore was in clear view.

A sound made Sabine turn. Cullen stood at the top of the basement stairs, gun still tucked into the black pants, watching her. Next to him, stairs led to a second level. She engaged the safety on her pistol and headed there. Climbing the stairs, she heard him follow.

Straight ahead at the top of the stairs, a hall led to three dark rooms. Sabine's hand trailed along the round ball at the end of the railing as she stepped into a room to her right. An unmade and otherwise unadorned mattress was the only piece of furniture other than a card table, where a black briefcase was open. A cord trailed from the briefcase to a plug in the wall. Inside the briefcase was a small monitor surrounded by other electronics. The monitor blinked a red "Camera 2" along with an unobtrusive beeping sound.

Cullen had been spying on her.

"It's infrared."

She turned to see him standing at the top of the stairs.

"For motion detection," he added.

She barely heard him. He'd come for her. He'd come, despite the risk of exposure. Why? A warm rush of hope threatened her resolve to keep him out of her heart.

He moved toward her, those eyes glowing with answering heat. "It isn't over, Sabine."

It took her a few seconds to realize he wasn't referring to the two of them. Just when she was beginning to feel strong again, he had to show up and knock her off balance. He was like one of her misguided achievements. She'd have to sacrifice too much of herself to have him, even for a little while.

"Did my father send you?" she asked.

He stopped too close. "No."

"I don't believe you."

"He didn't want me to come."

His eyes lowered and she felt his gaze like a physical touch, lingering on her chest. Then all that energy captured her with an unspoken message. She couldn't look away. Her pulse warmed with the shift of his gaze into hers. She flinched when he touched her hand, but his fingers only took hold of the gun. Letting him have it, she rubbed her arms and watched him tuck it in the back of his pants.

"I'll take you home."

From downstairs, the sound of something clanging to the floor ended the argument. Cullen ran down the stairs and Sabine followed. She heard glass shattering. At the bottom of the basement steps, she saw Cullen standing with his gun aimed out the basement window. It was broken, and the man who'd been hanging by the chain was gone.

Chapter 8

"While you're wearing the stain off my wood floor, I'll be downstairs stocking my shelves." Holding a fresh container of sun tea in one hand and a small cooler of ice in the other, she waited for Cullen to stop pacing in the middle of the living room to look at her. He'd seen her safely home in the wee hours of morning, just before Minivan Man arrived for his shift. Early. Now Cullen was trapped here, although he'd cracked a smile at her name for the reporter.

He didn't respond, but his impatience etched stern lines on his face. It was almost comical. "You don't do well with nothing to keep you occupied, do you."

His brow put a deeper crease above his nose.

Smiling, she opened the door leading to the stairs and quipped, "I'll send you a bill for the floor."

Stepping onto the first stair, she closed the door on his slightly less brooding face. Downstairs, the blinds were open in her bookstore. The sun was shining this morning, and there wasn't a cloud in the sky. It perked up her mood. She put the jug of iced tea on the checkout counter. She'd keep the Closed sign up and front door locked just in case Minivan Man decided to try to corner her.

Finding a plastic cup on one of the shelves behind the checkout counter, she put ice in it and filled it with tea. The sound of boots thudding a slow tread made her look toward the row of shelves that blocked her view of the office. Cullen appeared in one of the aisles. She'd known he wouldn't be able to stay upstairs with nothing to do. Pulling out another cup, she poured him a glass of tea. He stopped and lifted it from the counter when she finished.

"Thanks."

Sipping, he eyed the windows at the front of the store and started to go there.

"I want the blinds open," she warned him.

He didn't stop.

"I like the sunlight," she raised her voice.

He reached for the string hanging from the blinds nearest the door, heedless of the demand in her tone. Pulling, he lowered the blinds over the window.

"Leave the damn blinds open!"

Paying her no heed, he moved to the second set and shut them, plunging the bookstore into gloomy light.

Pursing her lips tightly with the rise of temper, she left her tea on the counter and stomped to the front of the store. She jerked the first blinds open. When she reached for the second one, his fingers slid around her wrist and stopped her. His touch along with his nearness kept her from yanking away.

"We'll leave one open," he compromised.

She watched his lips form the raspy words, disarming the rest of her temper. Those gray eyes held hers with heat that he tried to subdue with a slow blink, telling her he also felt the chemistry mixing between them. Slipping her wrist free, she went to a box of unpacked books and struggled to regain composure.

Cullen followed, setting his cup of tea on a table between two Victorian chairs in front of a gas fireplace. She tried to convince herself this was no big deal. So her rescuer was here in her bookstore. Did she have to fall all over him? No. Did she want to? No.

Yeah, right. She sneaked a look at his tall, cut body.

"I was surprised when I heard you were opening a bookstore," he said without looking at her. He was opening another box of books.

"Why?"

"You decided to give up your career?"

She stilled in the act of pulling some biographies from a box. "I didn't give up."

"I meant," he amended, "not many people could come back from what you went through and start their own business."

She straightened from the box and began slipping biographies on a shelf. "You're in Roaring Creek, Cullen. Don't act like I've invested in a franchise."

He moved closer to her and put some books on the shelf. "It doesn't have to be a franchise."

She let go of the last biography and slid her gaze to him. "Doesn't it?"

"I only wondered why a bookstore."

"I gave up an exciting hydrogeology career to open a boring old bookstore in a little mountain town. Do you think that's taking a step backward?"

"No. I think you took that job in Afghanistan to prove something to your father."

She flinched at his accurate assessment.

He half grinned. "It doesn't take much to see it, Sabine. When

he was young, he was never around, used your mother, had a
thing for thrills. It made you feel unwanted."

Swallowing, she faced the biographies. "That isn't importan
to me anymore."

"Your father's changed since then."

Grunting her cynicism, Sabine bent to the box of books, a
jerky, awkward movement. Why did what he say bother her s
much? It wasn't important to her what her father thought or felt
And she was living for herself now, not anyone else. This book
store proved it.

Cullen opened another box. Her first glance turned int
another. It was the one that contained some of her Pulitzer priz
winners. Her favorites. And his hands were on them. Trying t
ignore what that did to her, she put more biographies on the shelf

"They go on the shelf by author name," she said.

"I've been in bookstores before," he answered.

She couldn't resist a sassy remark. "For what? GI Jo
books?"

He laughed once and not very loud.

"*Playboy*?" She placed another biography on the shelf
sending him a slanted look as he carried a few books to the shel
beside her.

"The last time I bought one of those I was sixteen years old an
nervous about a date with the first girl I ever slept with." His voic
was deadpan, but she knew he was only playing along with her.

"Did it help?" she teased, even though she was actuall
curious.

He put a few books on the top shelf, calm as could be. "Yo
ought to know."

She slid another book into place. "You weren't that good."

"That's not what I heard."

She looked at him and saw his lopsided grin in profile. '
didn't make any noise."

"The fact you don't remember says it all."

What had she done? Moaned? She didn't think she'd cried out…then she did remember…she had.

"Don't make fun of that. It isn't funny." She slid the last biography onto the shelf and didn't move her hand from the spine. Just stared at it while her heart filled with feelings she did not want.

"I know," he murmured. "I'm sorry."

He stacked the shelf with a few more books. After a moment, she joined him.

"You've got some good books in here," he said, holding up a book by John Kennedy Toole between them.

"How would you know?"

"I read this one." He glanced up at the shelf. "I've read a lot of these."

"*You* read *A Confederacy of Dunces*?" She put her hands on the edge of a shelf level with her face and she stared at him.

"Twice." He smiled, continuing to stack the shelf.

She didn't know what to say around her surprise. And that smile was disarming.

"I like the author's view of people and society."

"He hated them."

"He understood their idiosyncrasies. Too well. It's a shame he committed suicide," he said.

Her curiosity got the better of her. "What other books have you read?"

Lowering his hands, he shrugged and turned in two little steps to face her. "A little of everything. The classics. Action or adventure. Thrillers. I like nonfiction, too."

"For a knuckle dragger you sure are well read."

A chuckle rumbled from him. "I started reading a lot when I was in college."

"When did you have time to read?"

"I made time. I like to read."

It seemed so unlike him. "What happened that you ended up working as a mercenary?"

"I'm not a mercenary."

"How do you know my father, then? Why did he hire you?"

His expression closed and she knew they'd reached an area he couldn't, or wouldn't, talk about. Disappointed, angry for being disappointed, because that meant she actually cared, she went to a box and got a few more books, jamming them into place on a shelf.

"Your father and I are just friends," he said.

"All his friends have secret lives. It makes perfect sense."

"Would you rather the whole town knew I was here and destroy everything I've worked for?"

Finished with the books, she folded her arms and cocked her head. "If it would help me get rid of you, sure. But somehow I don't think that's what would happen."

"You probably like it that I'm trapped in this bookstore."

"I didn't invite you here."

He stared at her a long time, unable or unwilling to argue. It was enough to tell her what had driven him to come to Roaring Creek. She straightened her head as memory rushed forward, taking her back to the pension, to the way he'd held her while she cried, the way he'd gradually responded to her kisses. His gentleness. His skin against hers.

As if sharing the memory, his eyes began to smolder with hunger. Undercurrents fired between them. She itched to pull him against her.

"I didn't need an invitation," he said. His raspy voice touched a place in her that hadn't been touched since Kárpathos.

She struggled against the temptation to let down her guard. "You make it sound as if that night in Greece meant something."

"Didn't it?"

Oh, it was getting warm in here. Her hands tightened on her

arms where they were folded. "I thought guys like you didn't get tangled in long relationships."

"Is that what you want? A relationship?"

"Have you ever had a relationship with a woman?"

He half laughed. "Of course."

"What qualifies as a relationship to you? A one-night stand?"

"No. One that lasts at least a few months."

That she hadn't expected. "When's the last time you had one of those?"

"In college."

"You're thirty-five. Don't you ever want to get married?"

"Maybe. Someday."

Maybe. But it wasn't important enough to make him worry much. Kárpathos hadn't been important enough. It had been important enough to make him want to protect her, but not enough for a real relationship. That hurt. Annoyed by her reaction, not wanting to start having fantasies of him in a relationship with her, she resumed stacking the shelf.

"What about you?"

She didn't turn to look at him. "We're finished with this conversation."

"It's only fair that you answer the same questions you asked me…and I answered."

The mischievous glint in his eyes said he was enjoying this.

"All right, what do you want to know?" she asked.

He braced his hand on the shelf, leaning closer, eyes glowing. "When's the last time you had a relationship?"

"Last year."

"How long did it last? Who was he?" He didn't seem so mischievous now. He looked…jealous. No, it couldn't be that.

But she smiled and said, "Almost a year. He was another geologist."

"Did you love him?"

"I liked him. A lot."

"Why did it end between you?"

"I realized I didn't love him."

He took his time responding. "Do you ever want to get married?"

"Of course."

"When?"

"When I fall in love."

The bookstore grew uncomfortably quiet. Cullen looked as if she'd said something frightening…and she felt she had.

A knock interrupted them. Sabine was grateful for it and started to go answer the back door. Cullen stopped her with his hand on her upper arm. She followed to where she could see into the office and watched him ask who it was.

"Noah," the voice answered.

Realizing she wasn't disappointed to learn he was here, Sabine gritted her teeth.

Cullen let Noah inside with a wary glance at Sabine. She looked like a tightly wound spring, the reaction to seeing her father compounded by her earlier mention of love. The way she'd said it kept ringing through his head. He was still fighting a cold sweat. Love? With Sabine, there'd be nothing comfortable about it. He'd lose himself in her. The very thing that had destroyed his father.

He caught the way Sabine watched Noah as he came farther into the office. She seemed wary and stiff, but the animosity he'd seen in her before was missing. Maybe she was starting to see that Noah wasn't the dishonorable man she'd once perceived.

"Did you find something?" she asked her father.

He nodded grimly. "More about Isma'il." He looked at Cullen. "I think his reason for kidnapping Sabine and Samuel had something to do with emeralds."

"What makes you think that?" Cullen asked. Finally, they were getting somewhere.

"When we found some villagers to question, none of them could identify the men in the pictures, but they were able to confirm Isma'il took over an emerald mine by force and was paying someone to fly gems to a dealer in Peshawar, Pakistan."

"You think Isma'il was smuggling gems into Peshawar? How is that linked to Sabine's kidnapping?"

"Someone must have crossed him. I'm guessing that someone is one or both of the men in that photo. And Aden might have known them." He looked at Sabine. "Did you know about the emerald mines when you were working there?"

Slowly, as if struggling to absorb it all, she nodded. "Everyone did. But we were there to assess groundwater conditions, not the potential mineral resources of the area."

"So no one had any reason to suspect Aden may have been working with Isma'il? Samuel never said anything?"

At Noah's question, Sabine's eyes took on that haunted look. She shook her head. "Nothing significant."

"He must have known what Aden was up to. And if he hadn't been kidnapped, Aden might have tried to kill him anyway." Noah looked at Cullen. "One of the villagers my men questioned was a friend of Isma'il's. He said Isma'il met Aden on a regular basis. They were doing business together."

Sabine made a choked sound and that haunted look intensified.

"I'm sorry, Sabine," Noah said to her. "I know this is hard for you."

She shook her head unsteadily. "No…I'm all right."

Cullen didn't believe that. She was terribly upset. While he could understand that, he had a feeling something more bothered her.

"Did your captors ever say anything about the emerald mines?" Noah asked. "Did they bring up Aden's name at all?"

She didn't seem to hear the question, just stared at some point between him and Noah.

"Sabine?"

Her eyes moved to look at Noah.

He repeated his question, and Cullen wondered what had her so spooked.

"No," she finally said.

Noah's mouth pressed in a grim line as he looked from Sabine to Cullen. "The only other person who can tell us anything about Aden is missing."

"Who?"

"My secretary. She's been gone for a few days now. I'm sorry, Cullen. You were right. I had Cindy's house searched and found copies of handwritten notes about your mission in an envelope addressed to her. If Aden was working with Isma'il, he could have persuaded her to give him the information and then threatened her to keep quiet."

Cullen's jaw tensed and his fists tightened with the thought of the men who'd lost their lives because of Noah's secretary. "How did you know it was her?"

"A reporter coerced Sabine to do the *Current Events* interview by agreeing not to expose her rescuer. Aden must have decided his mole talking to the press was too much of a risk, even with his threats."

Cullen didn't miss the revelation that Sabine had done the interview to protect him. It reached into his heart and warmed him. "So he makes her disappear before anyone can talk to her."

"And tries to kill Sabine in case she pieces together something damaging about her kidnapping."

"There has to be more," Sabine said. "Aden is afraid of more than being linked to my kidnapping."

"I'd have to agree," Noah said. "And those men in that photo might tell us what that is."

"Odie is working on that," Cullen said.

Noah nodded. "I'll let you know when I find out more." He started toward the door, stopping when he reached it to look back at Sabine. "Mae is cooking dinner tomorrow night. Will you be there?"

That snapped Sabine to attention. She straightened. "She didn't tell me."

"She asked me to let you know." He looked at his daughter with a silent message in his eyes. He was trying to make inroads with her.

Sabine's eyes hardened, her defenses building again.

"What time should we be there?" Cullen asked, earning a narrow-eyed glare from Sabine.

Noah looked relieved. "Six o'clock." With one more hopeful glance at Sabine, he left. The office door closed behind him, leaving Cullen alone with her.

"You didn't have to do that," she said, marching back into the bookstore.

Following, he deliberately ignored her mood. "There's something you aren't telling me about Aden."

She stopped, folding her arms in a defiant stance. He moved in front of her, unable to help noticing how her arms plumped her breasts.

"Yeah? Well, how does it feel?" she asked.

He'd take a little sass from her, considering what she'd learned today. "Do you know something that will help us end this?"

She put one leg forward, hips cocked. "Tell me your last name."

"McQueen."

Silence. He knew he'd just surprised her with his quick reply. Actually, he'd surprised himself.

"Are you lying?" she finally asked.

Fearing his heart was going to overrule his better judgment

this time, he answered anyway. "No. My name is Cullen McQueen. I have a house in Virginia. My uncle lives in Montana. He owns a ranch there. That's where I was before I came here."

Her fingers relaxed where they curved over her arms, and her eyes softened. "Not married. No kids," she said in an intimate whisper.

She transported him back to Kárpathos, when they'd said the same words to each other. Except this time the meaning went so much deeper. Last time she'd said it to mock him. Now it told him she felt he was giving her more of him. Not keeping so many secrets. It was a dangerous path for him to follow. In more ways than one.

"Not married. No kids," he said in return.

Her eyes softened further, and he let himself fall into her gaze for a while.

"I saw Aden meet with a man just before we were kidnapped," she said, that haunted look returning, growing stronger with each passing second. "I saw only the back of the man's head."

Cullen waited for her to continue.

"I keep having dreams of a monster who does terrible things. In the dream, I see the back of the monster's head. When he turns, his face becomes Isma'il's."

It supported what Noah had just told them. "I'm sorry, Sabine." If there was a way he could take away the pain that must cause her, he would.

"I didn't want it to be true," she said.

Anguish gave her voice a quiver. But she held herself together. It couldn't be easy knowing the man she'd watched kill Samuel was friendly with her employer, that her employer had known all along the reason they were kidnapped, that it could have been prevented. Maybe Sabine even thought she could have done something, had she only known whom Aden had met the day she'd seen him.

He moved toward her, pulling her against him and holding her while she struggled to keep from crying. She put her hands on his chest and he felt her sag against him, welcoming the offer of comfort. The last time he'd done this it had led to more. He tried to steel himself against the memory, but it circled his senses, luring him into its spell.

When her breathing slowed and tiny shudders of emotion died, she flexed her fingers. She was growing more aware of him, like he was of her, soft and molded against him. She leaned her head back and he looked down at her.

The desire to kiss her swarmed over him. Her gaze fell to his mouth. He felt the heat inside him kick up a few degrees. Her eyes met his, coherency returning, then going round with alarm. She pushed his chest and stepped back.

He couldn't help looking at her. At the faded jeans that showcased long thighs, at the plain but feminine white T-shirt that did the same and more to her breasts. Her small waist. Long red hair. Green eyes. He felt starved of her.

"I-I'm going to…to go upstairs…for a while," she stammered.

He watched her hurry from the bookstore, glad that at least she still had a hold of her senses.

Chapter 9

Steam from boiling potatoes on her mother's stove fogged Sabine's view of Cullen. He sat on one of Mae's plaid green chairs in the living room, surrounded by refurbished antiques and a river-rock fireplace. Cabin architecture and her mother's decorative charm made for warm atmosphere. Warmer with Cullen in the midst.

In a black long-sleeved T-shirt that flattered his chest and arms, he made it hard for her to concentrate. Ever since he'd held her the day before, things felt awkward between them. The way he looked at her. The way he noticed her looking at him. Something had shifted between them, and it tested her resolve.

Noah sat on the couch beside him. Cullen's gaze moved and caught hers. There it was again. That spark. She felt the heat sweep through her. Noah was still talking, but she didn't think Cullen was listening. Maybe she shouldn't have worn this little black dress.

"Are you mad at me?"

Sabine almost jumped when her mother came back into the kitchen. She'd just finished setting the rugged pine table adjacent to the living room.

"No," she said, trying to figure out why she'd asked.

"I didn't want to force this dinner on you, but Noah wanted it so much…." Her mother let the sentence silently end.

Noah had tried to strike up a conversation with her twice thus far, but she'd found a way to avoid him both times. He'd finally given up and gone to sit in the living room with Cullen.

"He can be persuasive when he wants to get his way," Sabine said, defenses pricking her.

"I agreed with him. It's time to put the past behind you, baby girl."

"That's a little hard after thirty-three years. I don't know the man and I have no desire to."

"I don't think you really believe that. He's your father."

"Biologically."

"Sabine, he's changed since he was younger. And I'm afraid I'm as much to blame as him for the way you perceive him."

She watched her mother pour iced tea into four glasses. "He was never here. What am I missing?"

Mae put the pitcher of iced tea down and looked at Sabine. "I refused to marry him because he was a mercenary who didn't want to live in Roaring Creek."

"You were right."

"No, I wasn't. Not completely. Deep down, he was always a good man."

What had softened her mother toward Noah? Sabine wasn't comfortable giving him the same consideration.

Disconcerted, she looked to where her father sat with Cullen. Cullen saw her and those hungry gray eyes drew her attention. She wished she could see the detail of them, their energy, the way she was beginning to learn their subtleties. Heat flickered and spread into a wildfire before she could stop it.

"Wow," her mother said. "He looks like he's ready to drag you back to your bookstore."

Not expecting her to notice so much, Sabine remained cautiously silent.

"Maybe I was wrong about the two of you," Mae went on. "When I saw that picture in the paper, I was so afraid you were going to fall in love with the wrong man just like I did."

Okay, it was time to take the focus off her and Cullen. "You don't seem to think Noah is wrong for you."

"There's a lot you don't understand, Sabine. I loved your father for a lot of years, but it's too late for us."

"Too late?"

Mae hesitated. She held Sabine's gaze. "I met someone after you left for Afghanistan."

"You *met* someone?"

"He's a rancher who moved here a few months ago."

Sabine struggled to wrap her mind around her mother being interested in someone other than Noah.

"Is it so hard to believe?" her mother asked, teasing.

"No. I'm happy for you."

"For the wrong reason."

"No, I—"

Mae handed her two glasses of iced tea. "Put those on the table. We're ready to eat."

All right. She'd try to give her father a chance. But only for her mother. Taking all four glasses to the table, she avoided looking at Cullen as he and Noah sat at the table. Sitting beside her mother, too aware of Cullen across from her, she glanced at Noah. He gave her a hesitant smile. She struggled with that old hope and avoided looking at both men. Only the sound of silverware against dishes filled the open room of the cabin.

Sabine picked at her food.

"You're doing a fine job with that bookstore," Noah commented, breaking the awkward silence. "Cullen said you were going to sell coffee, too."

She couldn't just turn off all the resentment she felt. Did he expect her to? She looked down at her plate and didn't respond.

When she looked up, it was to Cullen's softening eyes. No longer laced with desire, they silently encouraged her. He wanted her to forgive her father.

"Sabine was never the quitting kind," Mae said, adding to the small talk.

"We're having nice weather for this late in the fall, too," Sabine couldn't stop herself from saying. She couldn't pretend she wasn't still hurt by her father's desertion.

Noah met her smart remark with resignation. Long moments passed while he studied her, seeming to struggle with what to say.

"Sabine…" he began. She almost took pity on him. Finally, he gave up and just said, "You don't know what it did to me to almost lose you."

The honesty she heard in his tone and saw in his eyes grated against her defenses. She hadn't expected him to get so deep so quickly. "You're right. I don't know. Because I know nothing about you."

"What do you want to know? Ask me anything." More sincerity.

"You'll tell me?"

"Yes."

"Anything I ask?"

"Yes."

"All right. Why did you ask Cullen to rescue me?" Let's see how far he'd go with that one. She sent him a smug look.

Noah frowned his aggravation. Clearly, he knew where this was headed—somewhere Cullen couldn't, or wouldn't, want to go.

"It's okay," Cullen said. "I'll tell her."

Those gray eyes touched her, reaching past her surprise with purpose and certainty.

"Noah saved my life," he said, his voice warming her, the essence of him in it, strong and steady, full of honor and integrity. This was the man who'd rescued her, who'd held her in that helicopter and again in the pension on a little Greek island.

"You did it because you felt you owed him?" she had to force herself to ask.

"I was on a mission in Liberia. There were rebels rising against the government. They were part of a coup to overthrow the country's leader. My team was sent to take out a separate group of terrorists hiding there. What we didn't know was the Liberian government had hired Noah to send men to help fight the rebels. We were in a bad location, outnumbered and trapped by the rebels. Noah sent his team in to help us. If it hadn't been for that, everyone on my team, including me, wouldn't have made it."

She looked at her father. "So you cashed in on a favor?"

"Cullen is the only man I know who could do a mission like that," Noah said. "I wouldn't have asked if I'd had any other choice. And because Cullen is a man of honor, he agreed."

The fact that he chose that particular word knocked Sabine off balance. In everything Cullen did, honor drove him. But that honor didn't include her. Not beyond her rescue. How could she feel so much for a man who so resembled the kind she'd vowed never to love?

Love?

Panic billowed inside her. Where had that come from?

She found Cullen's eyes, saw the vitality that was becoming so familiar to her, a strength of character so few men possessed. It pushed her further off her axis.

"Do you work for Noah?" she asked, needing him to say it, to confirm it. "At all? Have you ever?"

"No."

"Who do you work for, then?"

He just looked at her.

"He can't tell you, Sabine. It's better you don't know, anyway."

She didn't acknowledge her father when he spoke, just held Cullen's gaze. "You lied to me when I asked you if my father sent you."

"I knew you were estranged from him."

"So you'd do anything, say anything, to get me to London, is that it?"

"To bring Noah's daughter to him alive? Yes, I would have done anything, said anything, to accomplish that."

The passion in his voice stopped her. Told her just how much his mission had mattered to him. More than she ever would. It crushed her. She felt the first sign of tears burning in her eyes and willed them away. No way could she cry now.

"All I can tell you is I'm a reservist," he said, a small crumb to placate what must be written all over her face. What a fool she'd been, falling for him like a lovesick teenager.

"What's your full-time job?" she asked, tossing it at him.

Defeat weighed the energy in his eyes. He couldn't tell her. She already knew he wouldn't.

Secrets were going to hurt her again. Just as they always had. Secrets had kept her from knowing the father she'd always longed to know, and secrets would keep her from knowing Cullen. What really stung was she wanted to know him. More than any other man she'd ever met. But nothing would move him to let her.

Putting her napkin onto the table, unable to take any more, she pushed her chair back and stood. "I want to go home now."

Now more than ever she understood why her defenses were so sharp. It was a layer of protection, something Afghanistan had stripped away, leaving bare the girl who yearned for a man to love her regardless of her achievements. The achievements were only a pretense. The girl underneath was real. Cullen had seen that girl after rescuing her. But it hadn't been enough. Like always, it was never enough.

After a stiff farewell to Noah and her mother, Sabine clutched her coat to her as Cullen drove down the mountain. She felt exposed. More unwanted than ever.

The truck stopped and Sabine saw that he'd parked behind his building. She opened the truck door and stepped down. The gravel seemed harder to navigate in high heels now that she didn't have her verve. All she wanted to do was go home and be alone. Anywhere as long as it was away from Cullen.

Heavier footfalls warned her he followed. She closed her eyes and leaned her head back, coming to a stop. There was no way she could outrun him in these shoes. Lord, how she didn't want to confront him right now.

"Sabine." He touched her arm with his hand as he came around to face her. She opened her eyes as he said, "I'm sorry."

Coldness gave her strength. She stepped back, out of his reach. "You're sorry."

"Yes."

Though his eyes revealed the truth behind the statement, she remained indifferent. "About what, Cullen? About who you are?"

"No."

"What, then?"

"You don't know what it would cost me."

"To trust me?"

"I trust you. I just…you don't understand." He averted his gaze.

She bristled that he was so adamant about protecting his

career. "You risk your life doing what you do. And for what? To be like *Noah Page?*" It went deeper than that, but right now she wanted to lash out at him.

"I'm nothing like Noah."

"That's not what I see. I see a man who holds his secrets dearer than the people around him. Noah does that. He did it to my mother. And me."

"Sabine." He moved closer and put his hands just above her elbows.

She saw the first sign of deeper emotion creep into his eyes. Though she braced herself, the heat of him seeped through her resolve. She took another step back, once again out of his reach. "I want you to leave Roaring Creek."

"I can't do that."

The way he said it told her he meant it. Despair swirled inside her. How much longer would her resistance to him last? How much longer before he broke her heart? She started walking toward the side of his building. Before she reached the street, he stopped her, pulling her around to face him.

"This isn't over yet," he said. "Someone is still trying to kill you."

"For you and me it's over. I don't need you to fight my battles for me." She pulled her arm free, stepped away and turned to walk briskly into the street. Didn't he see that she had to preserve herself? She needed a man who'd be there for her no matter what. She could not compromise on that. And Cullen was not that man.

His hand curled over her upper arm and forced her to slow. A tug made her fight for balance. She came against him in the middle of the street.

"I'm not leaving," he said gruffly.

"You've repaid your debt to my father. Go home. Go anywhere but near me."

"Damn it, Sabine." His hands slid up her arms and came to rest on the balls of her shoulders.

She put her hands on his chest. Feeling the hard muscle underneath, a flash of desperation rocked her. "Please, Cullen, don't make this harder than it already is." Emotion broke in her voice, all the desire she felt for him coming out, and the fear that she wouldn't be able to fight it much longer. She wanted to shut her eyes to the anguish in his.

"I can't," he said with equal emotion. "I can't leave you like this."

She did close her eyes then, overwhelmed by feelings more powerful than her will. His hands slid to her waist and he moved closer. She pressed her body against his, seeking to envelop herself in the invisible bond keeping them together.

He let his forehead rest against hers, and she stared up at his eyes, blurred so close to her own. She heard his breathing and realized she was breathless, too. He kissed her. Once. Twice. She wrapped her arms around his neck. He slid his hand to the small of her back and pulled her firmer to him. With his other hand, he cupped her head and kissed her deeper. From there this thing between them erupted. She strained to get more of him. He strained back. But it wasn't enough. She tipped her head back as his mouth planted wet, fevered kisses down her neck.

He lifted his head. Sabine opened her eyes to the ravaging hunger in his and knew she was falling hopelessly in love with him.

"Cullen," she breathed, wishing the thought had never come.

Hearing a sound, she felt him go still. He looked down the street. She followed his cooling gaze. A man stood twenty feet from them…holding a camera. He was snapping pictures of them. Cullen was facing the lens dead-on.

Cullen swore, pushing her away.

He stormed toward the reporter, who lowered his camera, then turned and ran. Minivan Man. At his minivan, he leaped inside, slammed the door and then the lock. Cullen tried to open the minivan's door, but it didn't budge. The reporter revved the engine, and the minivan rolled down the street toward Sabine. She turned as it passed by her.

Glancing at Cullen, she saw that he hadn't moved from where he stood in the street. It was hard for her to pity him when she had no idea what he was afraid the press would reveal about him. Knowing there was nothing she could say or do to make a difference, she walked toward her bookstore. Inside, she made her way upstairs, leaving the doors unlocked.

Several moments later she heard Cullen follow. The door to her apartment opened and she waited for his rage. But it never came. Instead of anger, she saw disbelief.

Closing the door behind him, he moved into her living room, where he sat on her sofa and bent forward to put his face in his hands.

Sabine relented and took pity on him. "You should leave town. Tonight. Now."

He didn't move.

"There will be more reporters by morning," she said.

"It won't matter," he answered, dropping his hands. "The damage is done."

"But—"

"It will only be a matter of time now."

Hearing the note of hopelessness in his tone, she lowered her eyes. She resented his secrets but she never meant to cause him pain. "I'm sorry."

She raised her eyes in time to see his gaze take in the bodice of her black dress, then travel lower before coming back to her face, his disgust with himself plain for her to see. It arrowed into the deepest regions of her heart.

Turning before he saw something she didn't want him to, she left him alone and went to her bedroom. She took her time changing into lounge pants and a matching shirt. Hearing him talk on the phone, she reluctantly went back to the main room.

"I'm sorry to call so late," he was saying as she came to a stop near the kitchen table. "I'm all right—" Whoever was on the other end of the connection must have cut him off. "Just listen, Odie. A Commander Birch will probably be calling sometime tomorrow. When he does, I need you to give him a number where he can reach me." He gave the person named Odie Sabine's phone number.

After a pause he said, "You'll know when you watch the news in the morning." Another pause. "Just give him the number. And if anyone asks you about SCS, tell them you have no comment." Sabine couldn't tell if the person named Odie was talking.

When he disconnected, he turned and saw Sabine standing there. She felt uncomfortable, as though she'd pried into his personal affairs. Then she caught herself putting his feelings ahead of her own. If the media exposed him, it wasn't her fault. Besides, she wanted to know what they'd have to say and it was the only way she'd find out. Cullen wouldn't tell her.

Since early that morning, Cullen had been watching the news, waiting for the break to come when someone figured out who he was. He found meager satisfaction that they weren't having an easy time of it. What really gnawed at him, though, was how the mystery heightened public fascination over his alleged romance with Sabine.

A sound made him look toward the hall. Sabine appeared, dressed in jeans and a white turtleneck sweater. The fact that the sight of her still stirred his desire annoyed him to no end. He knew what was underneath that sweater and inside those jeans. It was the candy that made him careless enough to send his entire life into chaos.

She moved farther into the room. Sweet candy. Irresistible sugar to his senses. His temper simmered hotter—at himself, not her. For letting her get to him the way she did.

He watched her fold her arms as she moved closer to the television. She looked tentative and he wondered if she was curious of what the news would reveal about him. When she saw there was a commercial playing, she turned and went into the kitchen.

He listened to her pour a cup of coffee from the pot he'd just brewed. Moments later a local news break began. Sabine came into the living room, sending him a wary but stoic glance.

Pretty soon she'd know everything. He wasn't sure how he felt about that. Angry with himself, for sure. Disconcerted. Maybe even a little nervous.

"Little is known about the man who rescued Sabine O'Clery from what appears to be terrorists in Afghanistan," the anchorwoman began, "but one thing is clear—he's resurfaced in Roaring Creek, Colorado, O'Clery's remote mountain hometown."

A picture of Cullen looking right at the camera appeared on the screen.

"Aside from photographs and O'Clery's claim he's from the United States, her rescuer's identity remains a closely guarded secret. Sources from the U.S. military continue to deny any involvement in O'Clery's rescue, and her father insists the man shown in this photo doesn't work for his private military firm, credited with arranging the mission.

"So who is this man who saved Sabine O'Clery's life?" The anchorwoman smiled. "Nobody seems to know."

Another photo appeared, this one of Cullen and Sabine kissing in the middle of the street.

"But whoever he is, the romance that started on a Greek island hasn't cooled. Is it love? And the question on everyone's mind—has O'Clery's rescuer resurfaced in response to her recent attack? George, can you tell us more?"

A live view of the reporter who'd photographed Cullen appeared on the screen.

"I saw Sabine O'Clery's rescuer come out from behind that building." The camera moved to show the building where Cullen had stayed. "Which is right across the street from O'Clery's bookstore." The camera returned to Minivan Man. "It isn't confirmed yet, but we think he's living there."

Cullen stood and went to the window to peer outside. He spotted Minivan Man in front of a camera and wanted to clamp his hands around the reporter's scrawny neck.

"As soon as he realized I was taking pictures of him, he came after me. I ran to my vehicle and barely had time to close and lock my door before he reached me. For a while there I thought he was going to tear the door off to get at me." The man laughed as though in awe and shook his head. "Wouldn't want to mess with that fellow. Not only was he mad, he looked like he could take down a tree with his bare hands. More than capable of rescuing a woman from a country like Afghanistan…."

Cullen smirked through the window.

Sabine's telephone rang. He spun in time to see her go to answer it. He strode toward the telephone. When she lifted the handset, he took it from her.

"Yeah."

"I'm looking at your face on television."

Cullen closed his eyes. It was the call he'd been dreading yet desperately hoping would never come. Tyler Birch. His army commander. Cullen gripped the phone tighter.

"Tell me you aren't the man who rescued Sabine O'Clery in Afghanistan. Tell me I'm mistaken."

Cullen didn't say anything. He opened his eyes and found himself looking at Sabine. He resented the sympathy he saw.

He didn't waste time or words. "You're not mistaken."

Birch cursed vividly three times. "What the hell is the matter with you? Does your duty mean nothing to you?"

"It means everything to me."

"Your actions don't show me that."

Arguing would only make this worse. Cullen said nothing.

"You've embarrassed me," Birch said. "And you've embarrassed the army. How do you expect us to answer questions from the press? One of our own carried out a mission in an unstable country without our knowledge. How do you think that makes us look?"

"I rescued a civilian."

"Yeah, and I'd like to know how. Where did you find the resources?"

Cullen couldn't answer that. Telling Birch his company was only a guise for something much bigger would jeopardize key people in the government who could not be exposed. If he had any hope of salvaging anything of his career, he had to play this very carefully. He hated the prospect of losing his position with the army, but if he had to, he would.

"Can't tell me, huh?" Birch said, anger growing in his tone. "Who's in on it with you? More of our own?" Birch laughed without humor. "That company of yours always did make me wonder. What are you hiding, McQueen?"

"I never intended to put you in a compromising position," he said, unable to say more.

A long silence carried over the line. "When I found out it was you kissing Sabine O'Clery at the London airport, I couldn't believe it. I thought the man in that photo looked familiar, but I didn't think you were stupid enough to do something like that."

Cullen felt himself go numb as he continued to look at Sabine. "I saved her life, sir."

"Don't you 'sir' me. What do you want? A medal?"

"She would have been killed if I hadn't done it."

"That doesn't change a thing. You went in there on your own, without army authorization. If you were more than a reservist, I'd court martial you."

"I didn't do anything wrong."

"Did you kill anyone while you were over there?"

Cullen didn't answer, because he had.

"If you did, you did plenty wrong. Those kills weren't sanctioned, McQueen. Some people will see that as murder."

Cullen turned his back to Sabine to hide his crumbling hope.

"You crossed the line. I'm going to initiate administrative action to have you discharged from the army."

Defeat made him drop his head. This could end everything he'd worked for, and there was nothing he could do to stop it. "I'm asking you to reconsider."

"There's nothing to reconsider. I've made my decision. You're finished, McQueen."

Birch disconnected before Cullen could protest.

He stood holding the phone to his ear awhile longer, unable to believe this happened. His commander didn't have to initiate administrative action against him. Birch couldn't court martial him as a reservist, but he did have a choice over whether or not to take administrative action. And he had made that choice. Cullen's Black Ops went deeper than even Birch knew, and that came as too much of a blow to his pride.

Hanging the handset back on its base, Cullen was glad his back was turned and Sabine couldn't see the depth of his angst. Losing his company was one thing, but losing his reputation with the army was unthinkable. There was no honor in a dismissal like the one Birch threatened. No integrity. How could he look back on this when he was an old man and not have regrets?

He turned then. Sabine stood with her arms folded protectively in front of her, her beautiful green eyes round and wide with concern and sympathy.

Letting her kiss him that first time had started all this. If he would have just stopped it, if he hadn't made love to her, maybe he wouldn't have felt compelled to come to her after hearing about her attack. And if he hadn't made love to her, he wouldn't have been caught kissing her in the middle of the street. He was so angry for losing control of his self-discipline. He should have known better. He should have seen this coming and stopped it.

Chapter 10

Another breaking news report sounded from the television. The corner of the screen filled with the face shot of Cullen.

He moved into the living room as the anchorwoman summarized what she'd said in previous reports. Then she started into the new information that must have been gathered through the morning. "Margaret Schlepp, a neighbor of Luc and Penny McQueen, has confirmed the identity of the man who rescued Sabine O'Clery from Afghanistan. Cullen McQueen is a reservist with the U.S. Army Special Operations Command in Fort Bragg, North Carolina, and he's anything but ordinary. His uncle, Luc McQueen, a well-respected retired army commander, has declined to comment on the heroic efforts of his nephew, but his neighbor had plenty to say." The screen showed an old woman standing on her front porch.

"I always thought it was strange the way they talked so proud of Luc's nephew when all they said he did was run a security temp agency somewhere in Virginia," Margaret Schlepp said, squinting under the Montana sun and showing missing front teeth. "SCS or something like that."

The woman had no idea of the damage she'd just done, Cullen thought, his spirits sinking to a new low. The name of his company was on the news. It was all over now. They knew who he was.

"The more we learn about this man, the better it gets," the anchorwoman quipped, smiling.

Sickened, he watched the screen fill with a view of his company in Alexandria, Virginia. The camera zoomed in on SCS's redbrick exterior and darkly tinted windows.

"With no advertisements describing its operation, no phone listings or evidence of a customer base, SCS appears to be much more than a simple temp agency. In fact, that seems to be the cover that hides its true purpose. Workers from neighboring businesses say they aren't familiar with the company or its founder and sole owner, Cullen McQueen. Few reported seeing employees enter and exit the building and couldn't identify McQueen as one of them. The SCS Agency is so secretive that it was difficult learning what the acronym stood for. Security Consulting Services sounds like a temp agency, but it's much more than that."

A video of Cullen's secretary waving away a cameraman and a reporter who followed her toward the entrance to SCS played on the television.

"Ms. Frank," a reporter called, "did your employer orchestrate the rescue mission that saved Sabine O'Clery's life?"

"No comment," Odelia answered harshly as she marched away.

"Did O'Clery's father hire your company to rescue her?"

Odelia opened the front door of SCS and disappeared inside.

The screen showed the anchorwoman again. "Odelia Frank might seem like an ordinary secretary to someone who walks through the bulletproof doors of SCS, but her background dispels any doubt as to the character of the company. Former J-3 Operations captain with the Joint Chiefs of Staff, Ms. Frank still holds her Top Secret security clearance and is an expert markswoman. This from an interview with her ex-husband." The screen went to a picture of a man sitting lazily on his living room couch, gloating as he revealed his ex-wife's expertise. A few minutes later, the screen switched back to a smiling anchorwoman. "With a secretary like that, there's little doubt the SCS Agency is capable of carrying out a rescue mission. We'll update you as we get more."

The anchorwoman turned to her coanchor, still smiling. "It seems Ms. O'Clery has caught herself quite a man."

"Yes, it does, Mary," the newsman beside her said. Then the man led the broadcast into the weather.

The telephone rang again. Sabine went to answer it on the third ring. When she hung up, Cullen knew it was a reporter calling. They had her phone number now.

He moved to the front window and watched the chaos building in front of Sabine's bookstore. The sight increased the weight of his situation. He was beginning to understand how his father had felt when his life had begun to crumble.

The telephone rang yet again.

Sabine answered and he heard the strain in her voice.

"I know. We just saw it." There was silence while she listened. "A reporter caught us when we got home after dinner last night." Pause. "Yes." Pause. "No." Pause. "I don't know." A longer pause. "All right."

Sabine hung up. "My father wants us to come to my mother's house. He said he can secure us from the media there. He can help us."

Realizing he did need help, probably for the first time in his life, Cullen sighed as he continued to look down at the growing

rong in front of Sabine's bookstore. His career with the army
ppeared to be over. His company could lose the covert govern-
ent support it needed to exist. He couldn't imagine what his
fe was going to be like without the things he'd worked so hard
 achieve. Lost in all this was the impact such a company had
 the fight against terrorism. American dignity. Freedom.
umanity. Everything that mattered most to him.

"All we need to do is get there."

Cullen turned. Holding a duffel bag in one hand and the keys
 her Jeep in the other, she looked wary of him.

Walking toward her, he reached for the keys in her hand.
'll drive."

She gave him the keys.

Downstairs, Cullen swung the back door open and marched
utside. Three reporters were on him in an instant.

"Mr. McQueen, can you tell us why you're here?"

"Do you suspect Sabine's attack is related to her kidnapping
 Afghanistan?"

"Do you have any plans to marry the woman you rescued?"

Cameras pinged and snapped all around him. He grabbed the
earest one and yanked it to the ground, shattering it into pieces.

"Hey, you're going to pay for that!"

He leaned over the cameraman. "Make me."

"Cullen." Sabine's fingers curled over his biceps. "Let's go."

The cameraman's eyes were wide and he stepped back. Cullen
ent each of the others a threatening glance before he moved out
f Sabine's reach and climbed behind the wheel of the Jeep.
Vhen she closed the door on her side, he sprayed gravel driving
way.

Sabine moved to the dining room window of her mother's
abin. Through the large pane of glass, clouds painted the sky a
loomy gray, matching her mood. Last night the news had flour-

ished with images of Cullen destroying the reporter's camera, followed by his menacing "Make me" comment. Rather than painting him as a dangerous character who operated outside the law, they embellished the he-man quality of his reaction, making references to his size and fearlessness. It was all so ridiculous, particularly in light of the fact that they were crucifying a man's livelihood.

She never thought she'd be happy her father had access to men who could keep the reporters at bay. But this morning a helicopter had landed in the clearing near her mother's cabin and six men had filed out. They were now camped at the end of the driveway. Mercenaries were guarding them, and she was glad about that. Who would have thought?

Turning her head, she spotted Cullen sitting in a plaid living room chair, his body slouched against the back, eyes hard and looking right at her. She could almost hear his thoughts beaming across the room at her. *If only he hadn't been stranded with her on a Greek island. If only he hadn't made love with her. If only he hadn't kissed her in London.*

If only, if only.

Her father sat on the couch. He'd just finished talking on a radio with one of his men down at the end of the driveway. Her mother waited in the kitchen for another kettle of water to boil for tea. They were all waiting for Cullen's secretary to call.

Sighing, impatient and feeling trapped, Sabine moved to the couch and sat beside her father. He looked at her in surprise as he clipped his phone to his belt. From the chair, Cullen brooded.

He looked lazy slouched the way he was, legs spread, arms on the rests. Only his eyes moved, but she could feel the energy from them. His cell phone rang. He answered it as he stood, tall and big in dark blue jeans and a white button-up shirt. Sabine listened to him go into the sunroom next to the dining area.

"It's worse than I thought," her father said from beside her.

She turned to look at him, wondering what he meant. "Excuse me?"

"You and Cullen."

Realizing he'd been sitting there taking mental notes of her nd Cullen's behavior, Sabine felt her guard go up. "It's a little oon for a father-daughter talk." She couldn't even imagine them aving one.

"I've seen the way he looks at you," he said anyway. "I'm not blind man. He's on his way to making the same mistake I made vith your mother."

She really didn't want to have this conversation with him. But he said, "He blames me for what's happening."

"He doesn't blame you. He's angry with himself for allowing t to happen in the first place. I just hope he comes to his senses efore it's too late."

Sabine studied her father's profile and grew uncomfortable.)id he think Cullen felt that much for her? "Is he going to lose is company because of me?"

He turned to see her. "Whatever happens, it isn't your fault."

"Is he going to lose it?" she persisted.

"Maybe. He could also lose his position with the army."

She'd only caught Cullen's side of the conversation when e'd gotten the call from his commander. "But he rescued me. would have been slaughtered if it hadn't been for him."

"Unfortunately, that won't matter. Cullen is a weapon. The rmy can't afford to have a guy with his background running ogue missions in unstable countries like Afghanistan. It's a uge political risk."

Sabine was beginning to understand the magnitude of what :ullen had risked to free her. "It isn't fair."

"It might seem that way now."

She angled her head in question.

"Cullen needs to decide what he wants out of life. Is it Special

Ops and casual relationships, or is it more than that? This whole thing is going to force him to make up his mind. I just hope he makes the right decision."

"He'll never give up his career."

"Losing his company the way it's structured won't take that away from him. Neither will losing his position with the army. He might have to start over with a new company, maybe change his business strategy. Instead of dangerous clandestine missions he can move over to infrastructure security. He can teach governments and big businesses how to protect themselves against terror attacks. Or he could move into an intelligence role rather than an operative one and send other men just like him on the secret missions. He can do that from anywhere. He might travel a lot, but he could live wherever he wants."

"What kind of company is he losing?"

Noah chuckled. "Even I don't know that."

She searched his eyes to see if he was telling the truth.

"Cullen works through the government, Sabine. You don't have to question his integrity. But it would be infinitely more damaging to him if the identities of his contacts were revealed. That's why he couldn't risk saying anything to you. He has other people to protect. Think of the media surrounding your rescue."

Her heart splintered under the weight of warmth. Not only was her father talking to her without reservation, but also he was revealing things about Cullen that confirmed what she'd known from the first time he'd held her.

"How do you know all that?"

"I don't know much. I only know how the system works. And I know Cullen. He'll sacrifice what he has with the army reserves to protect the people who make his company possible."

And that was the very thing that would drive him away from her. Losing something like that. His honor along with it. She turned to stare at the fireplace. "Roaring Creek isn't enough of an adrenaline rush for him."

"It wasn't for me, either," Noah said from beside her. "But now I'm an old man and I know what a stupid mistake it was believing that."

"I just spoke with my secretary," another voice interrupted.

Sabine looked up to her right, where Cullen stood at the end of the couch. His face was dark with anger. How much had he heard of her conversation with Noah?

"Odie was able to ID the men in the photo from Samuel's field book." He looked directly at Sabine through a heavy pause. "One is Casey Lowe, a supply helicopter pilot Aden hired. The other is a Polish gems dealer who frequently buys smuggled emeralds in Peshawar and sells them to a Colombian miner, who passes them off as his."

Sabine stood and approached Cullen. "Then what are we still doing here? We have to go see Aden, and this time make him tell the truth."

Cullen put his hands on her arms, stopping her from passing him. "I'll take care of Aden. You'll stay where I think you'll be safest."

She sent him a warning look he wouldn't miss. If he thought he could just tuck her away somewhere... "And where might that be?"

"With me."

After boldly landing the helicopter in a hotel parking lot in south Denver, Noah's pilot waited for Sabine and Cullen to get far enough away before lifting off and flying back toward the mountains. Cullen carried his rucksack and her duffel bag and, beneath stares from everyone who saw the helicopter land and take off, led her to a bus stop not far from there. On the bus, Cullen forced her into the window seat of the first row. The whispers began. A young woman in her early twenties moved up the aisle and extended a notebook to Sabine.

"Can I have your autograph?"

Sabine smiled at her and took the pen she offered along with the notebook. She scrawled her name, then handed it back. The young woman didn't take them from her.

"Can I have yours, too?" she asked, looking at Cullen with unbridled awe.

Cullen took the notebook and pen from Sabine and thrust it toward the young woman without signing. She timidly took it from him and turned away. Sabine signed two more autographs but no one else asked Cullen for his. The look on his face was enough of a warning.

Cullen pulled her out of the seat at the next stop. They walked down 14th Street in downtown Denver and stopped close to the performing arts center. He was looking at a tall building to his left.

"Why are we here?" she asked, since he wasn't going to volunteer the information.

"Aden lives in that building. Brooks Tower."

She looked at the building, the upper floors visible from here. "Are we going to see him now?"

"Not yet."

Cullen took her hand and tugged her across the street. A doorman opened the door of Hotel Teatro, and Sabine found herself inside an old luxury hotel. Straight ahead, the lobby stretched to two elevators. Through a wide doorway to the left, Cullen led her to the front desk. He paid for a room, ignoring the attendant's curious looks at both of them. The man said nothing and gave them a card key.

Sabine stepped into the elevator ahead of Cullen, the door closing on a view of two bellmen's smiling faces. Following Cullen out of the elevator, she stopped with him at a room door.

She entered ahead of him, pausing in the narrow hallway to admire the spacious bathroom with large square tiles and a rain-style showerhead. Moving the rest of the way down the hall, she emerged into the bedroom. To her right, a dark wood desk separated an armoire and entertainment center. The room wasn't big, but it was elegant. To her left, a single bed was centered on the opposite wall. King-size—but there was only one bed.

She sent an accusatory look at Cullen. He ignored her, dropping his rucksack on the bed and removing a pair of binoculars.

"There's only one bed," she said.

He went to the window with the binoculars. "It was all they had left on this side of the building." He drew the heavy curtains open and lifted the binoculars.

"We aren't sharing a bed," she said.

"I'm not sleeping on the floor."

Her heart skittered faster. "Well, neither am I."

He lowered the binoculars and twisted to look at her. "Then we'll sleep on the same bed."

Despite her trepidation, a responding flutter tickled her. Needing a diversion, she kicked off her shoes and opened the entertainment center doors to turn on the television.

For the next three hours Cullen studied Brooks Tower, spying on what she had to assume was Aden's condo. Sabine found a movie to pass the time and was halfway through a second when he finally put the binoculars down and looked to where she leaned against the pillows on the bed. She lost interest in the movie. He seemed more relaxed now.

"Are you hungry?" he asked.

For you, she thought.

His eyes began to smolder in response to what he must see in her expression.

"Yes," she said.

She watched him control his rising interest. "I know a good seafood place near here."

"Good idea." She climbed off the bed. They needed to get out of this hotel room.

A short walk to Larimer Street brought them to Del Mar Crab House. Sabine followed Cullen down wide stairs. A smiling hostess—who didn't recognize them—seated them at a table near the bar. It wasn't very crowded at almost nine-thirty. Sabine looked around at the tables. A family of four sat at a table two down from them, and a couple sat across the aisle. There were two people sitting at the bar and three other tables occupied by small groups of people.

Sabine took in the brick walls with pictures. The restaurant was open and rectangular, like so many of the older buildings in downtown Denver. It smelled like seafood. Facing forward again, she noticed a candle in a glass container, glowing between her and Cullen. He watched her as he sipped his water. Being watched by him was an erotic experience. She leaned back and enjoyed the slow burn that took over his eyes. But only for a moment. Where would this lead if she allowed it to continue? With no small effort, she reined in the pleasure of his sultry appreciation.

"Be careful, Roaring Creek might start to look appealing to you," she teased.

"It already does."

He had to mean something other than what she'd like to think. "You'd climb the walls with nothing to do."

"I can think of one thing I'd like to do."

She half laughed, too nervous to trust him. "What? Fish?"

He didn't answer, not verbally anyway. His eyes said it all.

A spark of awareness rushed through her. She struggled to cover it. "If only you were a permanent resident."

That worked to cool his ardor well enough. She felt him

withdraw. It also reminded her that he didn't belong in Roaring Creek. She pretended to look around the restaurant, willing the sting of his subtle rejection down to a manageable level. His reaction proved he was the wrong man for her. How much more did she need to keep her distance? If only it were that easy.

The sound of a news program filtered into her musings. She turned to a television above the bar.

"More information has surfaced about the man who daringly rescued Sabine O'Clery from her captors in Afghanistan," the newswoman said, a big smile bursting onto her face. "This hero is one to remember. Although the army has repeatedly denied any claim McQueen was once a Delta Force soldier, fellow Ranger Anthony Timmons says otherwise."

The screen switched to a ruthlessly short-haired black man. "It was years ago, but he was my platoon leader. I remember him because he was a scary dude. Big and serious and good at everything he did. Got promoted to captain about the time he applied for Special Forces. Lost track of him after that. He just sort of, you know…disappeared."

"Disappeared?" the reporter interviewing him repeated.

"Yeah. Nobody knew where he went or what he was doing. I kept sayin' he joined Delta, but nobody'd believe me." He laughed. "Now he shows up on the news and people aren't in such a hurry to call me a liar. I didn't know he joined the reserves, but it makes sense, since he runs his own Ops company now."

"You know it's an Ops company? Do you mean Special Operations?" the reporter asked.

The camera changed to a view of both men. "I don't know it for fact, but with McQueen's background it don't take much of a stretch. That company is probably blacker than anybody will ever know…."

The interview ended and the newswoman's beaming face filled the screen again.

That's when the murmurs gathered momentum around them. The woman sitting with a man across the aisle from them said, "Oh my God, it's them. They're *here!*"

"Mommy, look," came from another table.

Watching Cullen's reaction, Sabine's heart broke for him. His livelihood was crumbling and there was nothing she could say or do to stop it. When she realized she wanted to, feelings warred inside her. How could she have ever thought of him as a mercenary? She could barely think of her father that way anymore. The truth frightened her because it tore down defenses when she needed them most.

Cullen stood, dropping several bills onto the table. "Let's go."

Sabine didn't protest. Nearly every eye in the restaurant was lasered on them.

Jogging to keep up with him, she braced herself for his stormy mood. His boots thudded on the sidewalk with each of his long strides. He didn't look at her once on the short walk back to their hotel. There, the doorman smiled and opened the door for them. She was grateful that he didn't say anything, if he'd recognized them. They rode the elevator alone.

It dinged on their floor and the doors slid open. Cullen preceded her into the hall. At the door to their room, he opened it and went in before her, going to stand in front of the window. Across the street and in the distance, the Brooks Tower loomed.

She felt so bad for him. "Cullen—"

"I'd rather not talk right now, Sabine," he interrupted, without turning.

Recognizing his need to be alone, she went into the bathroom to take a long shower. Knowing the truth about him had stripped away her defenses. Whatever his company did outside the army reserves, it was for the right cause. He was a hero through and through. How could she find the strength to stop feeling so much for him? She wanted him now more than ever. If only she believed she could have him. If only she believed he'd want her the same way.

Chapter 11

Cullen unfolded his body and stood up from the chair, irritated with his inability to ignore Sabine. She looked sweet and sexy in her nightgown as she warily made her way to the bed, smelling fresh from her shower. He picked up his ringing cell phone from the desk.

"Yeah."

"What are you doing to yourself, Cullen?" Odelia Frank said.

She must have seen the news and all it had revealed.

"Lining myself up for a career change," he joked with a bitter bite to his tone. "Did I forget to mention that? I'm sorry."

"You're going to lose everything over this. You do know that, don't you?"

"I had a feeling."

"What are you going to do?"

"They're hanging me by my balls, Odie. What do you expect me to do?"

All he heard was Odelia's breathing for a moment. "I don't understand you, Cullen. It's so unlike you to allow something like this to happen."

Cullen twisted his body to look at the reason he was in this situation. Sabine lay in bed, her eyes open and watching him, so beautiful that it gave his heart a warm pulse. "I'll just have to find a way to fix it."

There was a long silence on the line. "Since you're still in denial, let me spell it out for you. Without anonymity, SCS is finished. Like the bottom of a dry martini. All right? You can't run a company like this one as a celebrity."

The sourness in his stomach started an ache. Odelia was right. He couldn't run the kind of covert missions he ran and expect them to stay that way with the media following him everywhere. Even years from now, he'd risk the possibility of someone recognizing him at the wrong time. The senator, the two generals at the Pentagon and the colonel at U.S. Army Special Operations Command who made his company possible would all turn their backs without so much as a see-you-later. Contacting Cullen would be too risky. Even if he were able to protect their identities, he'd have no guarantee any of them would be willing to step forward and support a new company.

"What are you going to do?" Odelia asked again.

He couldn't imagine a life without the army or his company. Complete disconnection from Special Forces.

"I don't know. But don't worry, I'll make sure you're taken care of no matter what happens. You've been a critical part of the team, Odie. I wouldn't leave you out in the street."

"Don't get wishy-washy with me, Cullen. I can take care of myself."

He smiled a little, looking at Sabine again. Her thick red hair was spread out on the pillow, and her green eyes still watched him.

Holding the blankets up to her chin, sexy as all get-out. Despite everything, he still wanted her. More than before, probably.

Sabine propped herself up on her elbows while she listened to his side of the conversation, her breasts perky and free beneath the nightgown.

"Just a couple more things and you can get back to ruining your life with your future bride," Odie said.

"She's not my—"

"I got copies of Aden's bank statements," she said, cutting him off. "There were some peculiar, regular cash deposits."

"Yeah? What do you make of it?"

"The transactions aren't large enough to make it worth his while smuggling emeralds on his own, but maybe he was helping Isma'il in some way. Like providing the use of a mule."

"Lowe?"

"None other. He could have flown the gems into Peshawar for Aden, who could have paid him to make the trips. He always withdrew a lot of cash before his trips to Afghanistan."

"Except Lowe got greedy and stole a pricey bundle of emeralds for himself."

"Aden had to be in on it. And neither of them thought Isma'il would kidnap Samuel and Sabine, which explains why there was no communication from Isma'il. At least, not overtly. But he must have gotten a message to Aden."

"Who ignored it."

"Of course. They don't care about the contractors. Samuel was on to them. Sabine is with Samuel, so they assume she knows as much as he does."

"Or that Isma'il revealed his reason for kidnapping them during their captivity. To demand Aden give him back the emeralds."

"Either way."

"So Aden and Lowe wanted Isma'il to kill them."

Sabine's eyes drooped with sadness with his comment. He wished he could spare her this.

"And when you rescued Sabine, Lowe was ready with low-budget mercs."

"Compliments of Noah's secretary."

"Right."

"There has to be more. Nobody in the States is after Aden or Lowe. There's no evidence Aden got his share of the money from the emeralds, either. What are they so afraid of?"

"I'm working on that."

"You're an amazing woman, Odie. Have I told you how much I love you?"

"You're full of it, McQueen. Why do I put up with your ass?"

Cullen chuckled, catching the way Sabine watched him now. She was wary of the way he talked to Odie. "Because I put up with yours." He winked at Sabine.

Odie laughed while Sabine's lips curved with the hint of a smile. "At least you haven't lost your sense of humor."

"Ha, ha, ha."

"One more thing."

"Yeah?"

"Noah's secretary was killed in a car accident. Car went off the side of a mountain. There was a blurb on the news. Maybe you missed it."

"Car accident, huh?" He had missed the news on that. He'd been too wrapped up in his own downward-spiraling world.

"That's what they said."

"Call me when you find Lowe. I'd like to meet the man." He already knew where to find Aden, and now he couldn't wait for the encounter.

"You got it."

He ended the call and sat on the edge of the bed to remove his shoes.

"Who was that?" Sabine asked from behind him.

"My secretary."

"Oh," she exaggerated the word. "The J-3 captain, expert markswoman secretary."

He stood and faced her, liking the way she looked lying there all soft and warm. "She's good at her job. I'd trust her with anything. Including my life."

"So would I, as long as I don't have to fight her for you."

Heat dropped low in his abdomen. Was she doing that on purpose? Flirting with him again, like she had at the restaurant? He looked at her while he removed his clothes down to his underwear. The way she watched, the way her gaze roved over his body and then stayed on his face, moved him in a way that should scare him. Instead, he crawled onto the bed, caging her on his hands and knees. Her eyes widened as he took in her face.

"You don't have to fight anyone for me," he said.

She blinked once. Her lips parted slightly and her breasts elevated with a deeper breath. He bent his elbows to bring his mouth closer to hers, staring into her eyes while an inner struggle took place in his head. If he kissed her, he might not be able to stop. If he didn't stop, what then?

He'd lose himself in her. He'd fall in love with her. And not a comfortable love. With her it would be intense. Deep.

Life altering.

The cold shock of fear swept him. He jerked back from her mouth. Then rolled onto his back and stared at the ceiling.

A sound woke Sabine. Opening her eyes to a dimly lit room, she remembered where she was. The light came from the bathroom down the hall, but movement in the room made her lift her head. She blinked the sleep from her eyes, some of her hair falling in front of one eye as she spotted Cullen standing at the foot of the bed. Glancing at the clock, she saw only two hours had passed since they'd gone to bed.

She brushed the hair out of her face as she watched him load his pistol with a metallic click, anxiety bringing her fully awake. Dressed all in black, he looked much as he had the night she'd found him in her bookstore, which did something hot to her insides. The only thing missing was a mask.

Where was he going at such an hour, and what was he planning to do?

His eyes raised. Combat mode again.

Though the news report yesterday had painted him nothing less than an American hero, he looked dangerous right now.

"Where are you going?" she asked.

He shoved the gun in a holster against his left rib cage without answering.

Pushing the covers back, she crawled to the edge of the bed and sat on her folded legs. He picked up a hooded sweatshirt that zipped up the front and shrugged into it. When he zipped it halfway up his chest to cover his gun, he looked almost normal. Except for his height and general menacing appearance in black.

"I want you to wait here," he said.

He started to turn, but she rose up onto her knees and stopped him by gripping his sweatshirt.

Facing her, letting her pull him closer, his lower legs came against the mattress and gray eyes found hers.

"What if something happens to you?" Realizing she sounded like a worried lover, she lowered her eyes. What was the matter with her? He knew what he was doing. He got her out of Afghanistan. What made her think he couldn't handle downtown Denver?

He bent his head until she was forced to look at him. His eyes were soft above an unsmiling face. His gaze moved to her nightgown. She could feel him warming further, which disconcerted her because it warmed her, too. How close he'd come to kissing her enveloped her.

"Don't worry about me."

Trying to get a grip on herself, she released his sweatshirt. But she couldn't resist touching him, so she flattened her hands on his black top between the partially open zipper of the sweatshirt. As his chest muscles flexed underneath, heat flowed more freely in her.

"What are you going to do?" she asked.

He didn't answer. Instead he raised his hand and slid his fingers into her hair and around the back of her head. She stared up at him, into the burn of his eyes. His mouth came down. Pressed hard against hers. His other hand slid over her rear for a kneading caress that pulled her against him while he kissed her long and deep.

Too soon, he withdrew and stepped back. "Don't try to follow me."

At the threshold of the hallway, he looked back at her. "There's a gun on the nightstand. It's loaded. Use it if anyone other than me comes into this room. Don't open the door for anyone."

The door shut with a solid thud, and Sabine collapsed onto her back on the bed. She stretched her body, arms above her head, humming with desire, wishing he was back in the room. On top of her. Inside her.

Sabine was sick of looking out the window at Brooks Tower. Every once in a while, a car passed on the street below. Lights glimmered from buildings. She bit her thumbnail. What was taking him so long? What was he doing? She didn't like imagining him hurting Aden, but she suspected that's where he'd gone.

The sound of the door opening gave her a jolt. She scrambled for the gun on the nightstand and aimed it at the hallway. Heavy footfalls drew closer on the tile floor. Cullen's dark shape emerged, sending her heart skipping with more than relief. She lowered the gun and put it on the table beside the chair.

Cullen dropped a small duffel bag he hadn't had with him when he left and shrugged out of his sweatshirt. He unfastened his gun harness and put it on the desk. It sounded heavy. He moved toward her, his biceps and shoulders pronounced in the formfitting black top, his eyes on her like an urgent touch.

He stopped before her. "He told me everything."

"He stole emeralds with Lowe?" Somehow knowing it was true changed the way she felt. It was no longer speculation. Aden and Lowe had stolen emeralds, and that was why she and Samuel were kidnapped.

"Aden never wanted you and Samuel to get hurt. But he was most concerned about you. He warned Isma'il if anyone touched you, the gems would never be returned."

Was that why Samuel had been killed and not her? "But he never intended to give them back."

Cullen shook his head, his eyes still radiating warm intensity, with concern for how she'd take this news. "Lowe made that impossible. It was Lowe who put mercs in the helicopter that fired at us, and it was Lowe who had more waiting for us in Egypt. He forced Aden to use Envirotech's resources to make it all happen. He also knew Aden could keep him informed about the mission. Aden persuaded Noah's secretary to give him information because he had no other choice."

"But I thought… I thought Aden didn't want anyone hurt. Why did he help Lowe try to kill me? Why did he feel he was forced to do it?"

"Isma'il had a friend in Afghanistan's Ministry of Justice. Turns out that friend made some noise about wanting whoever stole three million in emeralds to pay for their crime. Aden was contracted by the U.S. government to help with the groundwater analyses in the Panjshir Valley. There was a Status-of-Forces

Agreement in place, but it didn't protect nonmilitary personnel if a crime was committed. Aden and Lowe are both civilians. If the Ministry of Justice learns they were the ones who stole the gems, Isma'il's friend could demand their extradition to face trial and the United States would have to comply."

"Because of the agreement."

"Yes."

Facing trial in Afghanistan as an American was a horror not unlike the one she'd survived. Aden and Lowe had plenty of incentive to make sure that never happened. Even if smuggling emeralds wasn't a capital offense in Afghanistan, the punishment could be severe.

"So when I start digging, Aden gets nervous and goes along with Lowe to kill me."

"Lowe saw the photo of you holding Samuel's field book. They looked for it near the borehole but never found it. Aden searched Samuel's things, but the field book wasn't there. He must have just missed the contractor who found it, and that contractor must have put it in the shipping box right after Aden searched it. Lowe sees you have it and hires an affordable gun to kill you. Aden is too afraid to interfere. He doesn't like the way Lowe operates, but he also doesn't want to face trial in Afghanistan. With all the press surrounding you, they had even more reason to worry about exposure. It wouldn't take much for Isma'il's friend to hear about who planned your kidnapping and why."

Was she supposed to sympathize with Aden? She found herself wishing they both had been caught. It was what they deserved. Because of them, Samuel had died a terrible death. It made her so angry. Aden may not have wanted anyone to get hurt, but people *had* gotten hurt. People had *died* because he'd helped Lowe do what he couldn't.

"Is he dead?" she asked.

"Who?"

"Aden. Did you kill him?" She knew she was being unreasonable, but the injustice of Samuel's death brought it out in her. For the first time since her abduction, she wanted to imagine someone being tortured. She wanted Aden and Lowe to suffer the way Samuel had.

"I didn't lay a hand on him," Cullen said in a gentle voice. And it reached through her angry emotions, showing her he understood her so well. He knew it was grief over Samuel that made her lash out like this. "I didn't have to. He wanted to tell me everything. I think he was glad to finally get it off his chest. It was almost as if he expected me to show up, to give him a reason to come clean. He never wanted Lowe to kill you, but neither did he want to face trial in Afghanistan, and Lowe threatened to turn him over to Isma'il's friend if he didn't help him."

She moved around him. At the table where she'd left the pistol, she picked it up. She handled the gun for a while, wondering if she had the nerve to go across the street and shoot Aden herself. Cullen put his hand around her wrist, stilling her.

"Killing him won't bring Samuel back," he said.

Slowly she looked up, struggling with a riot of emotions churning inside her. "Why didn't you kill him? Why didn't you kill a man who just stood aside and allowed a good man to be slowly and brutally tortured to death and others to die trying to save me?"

"He's not the one who deserves to die, Sabine."

But someone else was—she silently finished his unspoken thought. And he intended to hunt that man down. She nodded her understanding, satisfied that justice would be served. Samuel's death would be avenged.

Cullen moved to where he'd left the duffel bag. When he returned to stand in front of her, he handed it to her.

"What is this?"

"Open it."

She put it on the end of the bed and unzipped the top. Inside were several bundles of cash. Aden's share of the emeralds.

"Do whatever you want with it," Cullen said. "Burn it. Keep it. Do something Samuel would have liked with it. It doesn't matter. It's your decision."

She stared into the bag for a long time, but she already knew what she was going to do. She was going to give it to Lisandra. It wouldn't make anything right, but Samuel would have wanted to take care of his wife.

Late the next morning, Cullen put his finger to his lips when he opened the door to the room-service attendant. The graying dark-haired woman smiled and nodded. She eyed him as she carried a tray into the room. He wore only his jeans. Was she looking at his bare chest, or did she recognize him? He knew it was the latter when she saw Sabine sprawled sleeping on the king-size bed and her smile turned impish. Covered to her chin and curled on her side, Sabine looked rumpled and content beside the spot he'd vacated.

Setting the tray of fruit, omelets, toast and orange juice on the counter between the armoire and entertainment center, the woman faced Cullen with covert but obvious glances toward the bed. As though on cue, Sabine rolled onto her back with a moan. She sounded sexy as hell.

Clearing his throat, Cullen opened his wallet.

"You don't have to worry," the woman said. "No one will know you're here."

He paused in the act of pulling out two twenties to cover breakfast and a tip.

"The entire staff has strict orders not to say a word to anyone." She winked and looked at Sabine again, who had folded her arms over her head to enhance her appearance of a woman who was sleeping off a night of hot sex.

Cullen grinned and replaced the twenties with a hundred.

The woman thanked him profusely as she left.

Taking the tray to the end of the bed, he stopped and stared down at Sabine. Two things she loved since coming home from Afghanistan were food and sleep. He adored that about her. He had no idea why.

She made another sleepy sound as her eyes fluttered open and found him. It was all he could do to keep himself from crawling on top of her. She made it worse by rising onto her elbows, the blankets falling from her breasts and the strap of her nightgown slipping off one smooth shoulder.

"Good morning," he said.

She smiled sleepily up at him. "Same to you."

Did she know what she was doing to him? Cullen moved on his knees toward her. Sabine sat straighter, crossing and folding her legs as he placed the tray in front of her. He stretched onto his side beside her, bracing himself up by his elbow. He was very close to that bare shoulder.

Sabine lifted the carnation that someone had placed inside a small glass of water and brought it to her nose. Watching her smell the flower kept his interest stirred.

Lowering the flower, she turned her head toward him. He looked at her mouth.

"What are we going to do?" she asked, twirling the carnation in her fingers.

He could think of something, but that's not what she was asking. She wondered what they would do about Aden and his pilot. Taking the carnation from her fingers, he lifted it to her lips and used it to brush their soft fullness. "You're not doing anything."

Her lips parted and he saw the quickening of her pulse in her neck. Heard it in her breath. Then she wrapped her fingers around his. He let her take the carnation from him.

"Are you going to find Lowe?" she asked.

There went the mood. But it was just as well. He didn't want to give her false hope there was any kind of future for them. She couldn't do casual and he couldn't give her more. "Yes."

"And then what?"

He didn't answer, which for Sabine was the same as answering her question. She was getting to know him too well.

"You're going to kill him, aren't you."

He could see in her eyes that she didn't like the idea. Last night she was ready for blood, but today she was back to herself. While he couldn't blame her after what she'd endured in Afghanistan, it spurred his annoyance. Casey Lowe would kill her without a second thought. Sabine might think she could defend herself, but Cullen knew better.

"Lowe isn't going to get another chance to come after you, Sabine. I won't let him."

She didn't say anything, but he could tell he hadn't swayed her.

"I can't always be around to protect you."

That ignited green fire in her eyes. "No, you'll run away to your next mission and I'll be just an afterthought." She stabbed the carnation back into the glass of water and slid her legs over the side of the bed to stand. "God, I should have seen this a long time ago."

What did she mean, *run away?* He watched her stomp toward the bathroom, then propelled himself up off the bed to go after her.

"What do you want me to do? Let him get away with it?"

"No." She started to close the door.

He slapped a hand on it to stop her. "What do you want me to do?"

She met his eyes with the fiery energy of hers. "Can't you think of anything other than your missions? What's so frightening about having feelings for someone?"

"What?" Where had all this come from?

She moved forward, pressing her hands on his chest and giving him a shove. Perplexed, he let her back him against the wall.

"What are you so afraid of?" she whispered.

"I'm not afraid." He wished he knew what had her so riled.

She raised up onto her toes. Eyes alive with energy, she pressed her mouth to his. The shock of it stilled him. An instant later, it inflamed him.

He wrapped his arms around her, pulling her higher and tighter to him. Her tongue slid against his. He angled his head and took her deeper, cupping the back of her head with his hand. He felt every inch of her beautiful body against his.

All he'd have to do is turn and put her back against the wall, lift her nightgown and push his underwear down and he could assuage this maddening lust that wouldn't leave him alone. He could drive it out of his system. He started to do just that when she withdrew. She stepped back and he had no choice but to let her slip out of his arms.

"Do you want me?" she asked.

"Yes," he rasped.

"And then what?"

Realizing this was a continuation of their original dialogue, he scowled at her.

"You run off to your next mission," she said, answering her own question.

Because he was afraid. He got it now. He understood what she meant. He was afraid of the *then what*. Though it irritated him to be accused of that, he couldn't argue her point.

His cell phone started to ring, and he was glad to go answer it. He flicked on the television while he lifted his cell to his ear.

"You aren't going to believe this," Odie said.

He barely heard her. A breaking news report showed the front entrance of Brooks Tower, where police and emergency vehicles, lights flashing, were parked. A newswoman was in the middle of a sentence.

"…are no leads and no witnesses have come forth."

"Lowe is in Denver," Odie continued.

"Really." He said it sarcastically.

When Sabine got out of the shower, she realized she'd left her clothes in the other room. Wrapping a towel around her instead of putting the nightgown back on, she left the bathroom. It wouldn't take long to find something to wear. Just a minute or two. She tried not to think of Cullen's reaction to seeing her in only a towel, and ignored the lurking thought that maybe deep down she wanted him to see her like this. Her time in the shower had done little to cool what kissing him had brewed.

She emerged from the hall. Cullen held a pistol, pushing a clip into place. He wore jeans and nothing else. Those gray eyes lifted and saw her, then lowered to take a startled journey over the towel and everything it didn't cover. A fraction of a second later, heat wiped out any surprise.

She stopped halfway to her bag, her hand tightening on the towel as a flutter blossomed inside her. He stood as still as she did, his bare chest smooth over hard muscle, bent arms globing his biceps, holding the gun in his big hands. He reminded her of the way he was when he'd rescued her. Clearly her brain was muddled if she found the way he held a gun sexy.

He turned the safety on as she moved forward and came to a stop before him.

"Did something happen?" she asked.

"Lowe killed Aden after I left him last night."

That worked to dim the invisible chemistry flying between them. "How do you know?"

"Odie told me. And it was on the news."

"How did Lowe know you went to see Aden?"

"He must have seen me."

"Wouldn't you have noticed that?"

His mouth hitched up higher on one side. "I appreciate your confidence in me, but he's probably watching us from a building. I'm guessing The Curtis hotel. I'm waiting for a room number."

"How did Lowe know where to find us?" she asked.

"He didn't. But he knew we'd come to see Aden."

She looked toward the window where the drapes were drawn aside, not liking the idea of being watched. "Odie can get that room number for you?"

"If she can't, I will."

She turned back to him, wondering how long they'd be stuck in this room, alone. "What are we going to do?"

He paused. "Wait for Odie to call."

His hesitation and the warming embers in his gaze left her no doubt he was thinking the same as her. They were alone, with nothing to do but wait.

He looked down where the towel left the tops of her breasts bare. She wished she hadn't kissed him. More than helping her make a point, it fueled an already smoking passion.

This morning he'd turned a carnation into a sex toy. The last tether of control was a weak one. She felt it hover between them. Felt him want to finish what she'd started. She held the towel with both hands, as though it would keep her from letting him.

Without moving his eyes away from her, he leaned to his side to put the gun on the only table in the room. His muscled chest flexed and relaxed as he straightened, biceps pressing against his sides. He moved toward her and didn't stop until he stood close. She felt her forearms brush his skin. A lovely shiver raced through her.

Lifting his hand, he slid his fingers into her wet hair at the back of her neck. She couldn't breathe as his head came closer.

"I can't stop this anymore," he said, soft and raspy.

The words melted through her, so mirroring the way she felt. He kissed her. She shuddered with need and strained to take more of him. Angling his head, he opened his mouth over hers. She gave him all of her.

He curved his arm around her waist, drawing her fully against him. She let go of the towel to put her hands on him, loving the contour of muscle as she ran them up his body to bring her arms around his neck. The tickle of his hair on her skin, the warm force of his mouth on hers, his tongue making love with hers, the smell of him, it all wrapped around her senses and obliterated everything else. He gripped the towel behind her and pulled. She heard it fall to the floor. Her bare breasts pressed against him.

He lifted her and she folded her legs around him, kissing his mouth. This was so much more intense than in Kárpathos.

"I want you too much," he said against her kisses, stepping toward the bed.

The words sent emotion soaring in her heart. She kissed him, a way of answering without saying out loud the truth of what she felt. He took over the kiss, slanting his mouth over hers, meeting her passion and urging her for more.

Her back came against the mattress. She watched him straighten and jerk at the button and zipper of his jeans, push them down his legs and kick them aside. All the while he looked at her, hungry anticipation ablaze.

He crawled over rumpled blankets and sheets until he was on top of her. The feel of his body on hers amplified her yearning to have him inside her. He lowered himself onto his elbows, his face close above hers, eyes beaming a growing message of love. Oh, to believe and trust what she saw....

"Cullen," she said, sighing his name before his mouth came down to hers. She wanted to say more but held back.

He kissed her with all the force of his passion. And she met it with her own, telling him that way.

"Too much." He sounded breathless. She exulted in his confession, knowing he felt something deep, that it matched what she felt.

Trailing his lips from her mouth, he kissed her chin, her neck. His hands slid from her shoulders to her breasts. He kissed his way down, took a nipple into his mouth, then the other. His hands sank into the wet strands of her hair on the pillow. His breathing warmed her skin as he planted gentle, wet kisses along the slope of her breast, her ribs, her stomach. Then he reversed the journey, a silent reverence of unspoken love.

He moved up from her stomach and held himself over her. Those strong arms bent to bring his mouth to hers. She craved kissing him. Running her hands over his warm skin, she caressed the hardness of his muscled chest and abdomen, sliding around his trim waist to his smooth back. She kissed his cheek and chin, finding her way back to his mouth, sharing the salty taste with him.

He lifted away with a coarse breath and found her eyes with his. She died a tiny death as he slid into her. He pulled back for another wet, tight slide. She sought his mouth and he gave her another soul-moving kiss, pushing deep.

A shiver of building heat made her whisper his name again. It drew a ragged exhale from him. He kissed her hard and quick before he drove into her with more urgency. An insatiable ache gave way to spectacular sensation that spread everywhere in her body. Sabine heard her own guttural yell.

Cullen collapsed on top of her, his head resting beside hers. She trailed her hands down his back, letting them lie on his waist while they both caught their breath, never more at peace. Certain for the first time that no matter where this led, no matter what happened between them, she would never have any regrets.

Chapter 12

Sometime during the night Sabine woke to Cullen stirring. She moaned, remembering the afternoon they'd shared, most of it right here on this bed. Realizing he wasn't in bed with her anymore, she lifted her head and blinked her vision clear. Through the darkness she watched him shove his pistol into the holster strapped to him. He was dressed in black again. Alarm jarred her fully awake.

She sat up on the bed. "Cullen?"

He looked at her in that way of his. The soldier going out for a kill.

"Where are you going?" Of course, she already knew. But after what had transpired between them, she didn't want him to go anywhere. What if something happened to him? What if he was killed?

"Stay here, Sabine," he said, his eyes willing her to heed him.

"Don't go," she said.

He turned and moved toward the hall.

"Cullen." She couldn't stay here imagining him killing a man. Methodically. Intentionally. Choosing that over her. His mission. This is what he did. No. Her heart wrenched with a painful lurch.

"Please." If he left without acknowledging the way she felt, he'd lose her. She wouldn't compromise herself after this. It was time to take action where he was concerned. He either had to show her how much she meant to him or let her go.

Stopping at the threshold of the hall, he put his hand on the wall and turned his head to look at her. Seconds passed and then he dropped his hand, turning to face her.

"Sabine…"

"Don't go, Cullen." She shook her head. "Not tonight."

Even as he sighed, his eyes softened. Then warmed as he took in the sight of her naked above the blankets. He strode slowly to the side of the bed. Leaning over, he braced his hands on the mattress and brought his face close to hers.

"I have to do this," he said. "Odie called. I know where to find Lowe now. I have to go before I lose the chance."

She curled her fingers around the strap of his holster. "Don't, Cullen. If I matter to you at all, don't go."

His mouth formed a hard line with the pitch of his brow. "What do you want me to do? Let him live so he can come after you again?"

"This has nothing to do with Lowe. This has to do with you and me."

Cullen lifted his hand and cupped the side of her face. "I have to end it, Sabine."

She put her hand over his. "Not like this." Didn't he see? He would have sneaked out into the night without telling her where he was going. When he was on a mission, he tried too hard to shut her out of his mind. Well, this time she wouldn't let him. She wanted him to acknowledge his feelings for her—and hers for him. Just once.

As he stared at her, she could see him beginning to waver.

"Don't leave." She turned her face to kiss his palm. "Don't leave me."

A heavy breath sighed out of him, and he kneeled on the bed beside her. Taking her face in both hands, he kissed her. Sabine felt his heart in the way he moved his mouth over hers.

Stretching out beside her, he pulled her close and did as she asked. He stayed.

She slept. Content and warm. In the morning she woke to something hard digging into her ribs. She opened her eyes. Her hand rested on the rough material of Cullen's black top. The hard object was his gun. Raising her head, she saw that his eyes were still closed. His arm was around her, his hand over her hip. Her leg was between his.

He stayed.

Sabine studied his face while the meaning of that soaked through her, drenching her heart with love. His long dark lashes lay beneath his eyes and stubble colored his skin. His lips were soft with sleep.

She'd asked him to stay and he had. He'd chosen her over his mission.

She moved up and pressed her lips to his. Breath from his nose warmed her skin. His arm around her tightened. She rolled on top of him to avoid his gun. Straddling his hips, she smiled at the heat that grew in his sleepy eyes as he woke.

Leaning over, she kissed him. His hand came to the back of her head and held her there. She pulled back and crawled down his body. She kissed his stomach through his clothes then boldly kissed the hard bulge in his pants, taking her time there, dragging her tongue over the material that blocked her from him. She raised her eyes and saw that he'd lifted his head off the pillow to watch her. His features were fierce with desire.

She smiled at him and climbed off the bed.

"Where are you going?" he asked gruffly.

She laughed lightly. "I want to go shopping."

He sat up on the bed, quick as a big cat, and took her wrist. "Later."

Hooking her with his arm, he pulled her onto her back and rolled on top of her. He rose up on his knees and shrugged out of his gun holster. It thudded on the floor.

Sabine reached up and grabbed the black material of his shirt, pulling him down to her. He kissed her, smoothing her hair back from her face.

"See what you do to me," he rasped.

"Yes." She smiled against his mouth.

He chuckled, deeply and manly, vibrating against her stomach and chest. His laughter faded as he shifted his hips, the black material of his pants brushing against her bareness. She reached between their bodies and tugged at the button. It loosened while she looked up at him, into gray eyes full of an emotion she knew he wasn't ready to name. His breath rushed out and he took over the task, yanking his pants down over his hips. He kissed her and found her at the same time, every hard inch shoving into her wetness.

Sabine ran her hands over the black material of his shirt, reveling in the feel of hard muscle underneath. She continued over his shoulders and down to his chest. All the while he moved inside her, hard but slow. She closed her teeth over the muscle of his forearm through the material of his shirt as an incredible celebration of love burst between them.

Sabine walked beside Cullen on their way to dinner, worried by his mood. He seemed disturbed. While emotion burgeoned inside her, pushing to come out in words she longed to say, a wall seemed to be growing inside him. He'd chosen her over his mission, but he wasn't ready to call what they made together love. They'd spent the morning in bed and the afternoon shopping. No mention of Casey Lowe had been made, though Cullen carried his gun with him, hidden in his boot.

Passing the Paramount Cafe, Sabine heard '80s music and stopped to listen. People sat on a patio, in front of the old stone architecture of what once was the Paramount Theatre.

Cullen took her hand and led her to a table, and they ordered a light dinner. The old charm of the building relaxed her. After their dishes were cleared away and Cullen paid, he pushed back his chair and stood. Extending his hand, he said, "Let's go back to the hotel."

She knew what he'd do once he got there. Prepare to find Lowe. She couldn't explain her disappointment. Maybe somewhere deep inside she knew once he killed Lowe, his mission would be over, and so would they. Even after what they shared.

"I need to find a bathroom first," she said. The hotel was a long walk, and she didn't think she could wait.

He let her go. Down a hallway of terrazzo tile, she found a bathroom and went inside. She relieved herself, then bent over the sink after washing her hands to splash cool water on her face. Shutting off the water, she dried her face and hands and left the bathroom.

As soon as she entered the dim hall, she saw a flash of metal before something hard slammed against her head. Then everything went black.

Cullen stood near the edge of the patio where several people talked and laughed over dinner. The feelings swimming around in him made him edgy. He was so lost in Sabine he wondered if he'd ever be able to think coherently again. The media had destroyed his company and may have cost him his career with the army. His life was in chaos. Yet, all he could think about was her.

How had he come to feel so much for her? He didn't want to love her. Or was it too late?

Cullen felt the shock of the thought ripple through him. Did he love her? The intensity of their lovemaking said a lot to that end. Panic rushed him. No. He didn't love her. Not like that. He couldn't. He checked his watch as he paced in front of the building. What was taking her so long?

Suddenly, he froze. Jerking his head toward the building, he looked at the door Sabine had entered.

"No." He ran inside.

He searched for her but couldn't find her in the crowd. He hurried down a hall that was disturbingly dim and pushed the door to the women's restroom open. All the stalls were empty. No one was in the bathroom.

His heart slammed in his chest and his breathing grew erratic.

Back in the hall, he looked for another exit and found a door. Pushing through, he found himself in an alley. It was empty of people.

"Oh, God," he panted, running the opposite direction of 16th Street until he emerged in a parking lot.

Where had Lowe taken her? Cullen could only guess. He'd been so besotted with her, so caught up with the way she made him feel that he'd forgotten the danger.

Pulling his gun from his boot, his hands trembled as he slipped off the safety. This was like no other mission he'd experienced. He was scared. Really scared. Sabine…

What if she was already dead? He felt sick with the possibility. Lowe had no reason to wait to kill her.

"I can't lose her." His mind became a kaleidoscope of dread. If she died, it would kill him. Never before had he felt closer to knowing the agony that had destroyed his father.

Think.

The money. Maybe Lowe wouldn't kill her until he got Aden's share of the money. He clung to that thought as he ran to The Curtis. A car screeched around the corner behind him. When it passed, he spotted the driver. Blond hair.

Cullen started looking for a car to use.

Sabine drifted out of unconsciousness and opened her eyes to darkness. The sound of tires over a dirt road told her she was in a car. In the trunk of a car, suffocating and eerily familiar. Instantly she was back in Afghanistan. In her dark cell. Alone. Waiting to die.

Her heart pounded so hard she felt her pulse in her ears. Her frightened breaths surrounded her. Fear overwhelmed her, an otherworldly vapor that threatened to choke the strength out of her.

She squeezed her eyes shut. *Stop,* she ordered herself. *Stop it!* Fear would be her only adversary if she allowed it. She had a choice whether to give into fear or not.

Opening her eyes, she tried to see around her. It was too dark. She felt with her hands for some kind of weapon. There was nothing in the trunk.

The car came to a halt. Her heart raced faster. It was okay if it raced. She needed it to race. It was the fear she had to control.

Sabine adjusted her legs and mentally prepared herself to attack as soon as the trunk opened. The engine turned off and she listened to the car door open and close. Footsteps grew closer. A key slid into the lock. Turned. The trunk began to open.

Sabine pushed upward with her back, sending the trunk springing the rest of the way open. Lowe raised the gun. She registered his blond hair and glacial-blue eyes before she rammed her palm against his big nose. She recognized him from Samuel's picture.

Lowe stumbled back, holding his nose. Sabine jumped out of the trunk and ran. In the distance, cars moved along a busy street. Between that and her, an old farmhouse with dark windows stood perched on the bed of a truck, ready to be moved.

Lowe's gun exploded. He missed. She heard the bullet strike the ground far off its mark. She made it around to the other side of the truck before more bullets pinged against metal and wood. Peering around the back of the truck, she watched Lowe tread toward her. Looking up at the farmhouse on top of the truck, she spotted an open window. Climbing up onto the flatbed, seeing Lowe raise his gun and take aim, she hurried to pull herself over the windowsill.

She jerked as a bullet splintered the trim to her left, but she fell inside the house unharmed. Scrambling to her feet, she ran through a badly run-down bedroom, down a hall and into the front of the house. The front door was open a crack, but Lowe hadn't come inside yet. She heard something in the rear of the house. Her heart beat as fast as bird wings. She tried to quiet her breathing and looked for something to use as a weapon.

Cullen drove the Sebring he'd stolen onto a deserted road that connected to a busier one that led to Tower Road and Denver International Airport. By some miracle he'd managed to keep Lowe's car in sight. He'd gotten lucky, catching up to him after stealing the car.

Lowe had parked his car near an old farmhouse supported on the back of a truck. The trunk of the car was open, but there was no sign of Lowe. No sign of Sabine, either.

Cullen had to fight the dread electrifying his senses, force himself to remember he was trained for this.

Getting out of the Sebring, he ran toward Lowe's car. He searched his surroundings. Bare, flat ground. The house on a truck. Nothing moved. Lowe must have taken her into the farmhouse.

Holding his gun ready, he peered into the trunk. It was empty. Closing his eyes briefly, breathing through the light-headedness of relief that he hadn't found Sabine's body there, he moved toward the house.

Stay focused. Find Sabine. Kill Lowe.

At the front of the truck, behind the cab, he climbed onto the house's covered porch. The door was open a crack, and he could hear the sound of a struggle. He pushed the door open, aiming his weapon inside, wishing he had night-vision gear. Stepping inside, he moved to the end of the entry wall and carefully peered around it. In a badly maintained kitchen, Sabine swung a piece of floorboard trim at Lowe. Lowe blocked it and knocked it from her hands. It fell to the floor with a clatter. Cullen stepped into the open the same instant Lowe saw him. Instantly Lowe hooked his arm around Sabine's neck, hauling her against him and putting a pistol to her head. Sabine clawed at the arm that held her, her eyes seeing Cullen and staying on him with a silent plea.

Cullen's breath stopped and his heart felt near to doing the same. *Stay focused.*

He aimed for Lowe's head.

"Drop the gun or she's dead," Lowe said.

"Let her go."

Lowe shook his head, his eyes filling with anger. "I've about had it with you. Drop it now or I'll kill her."

Don't hesitate, Cullen told himself. *Shoot.* He wouldn't miss. He never missed. Not at this range.

"He wanted you to follow us here, Cullen," Sabine said.

Lowe gave her a jerk and tightened his hold. "Quiet!" To Cullen he repeated, "Drop the gun."

Sabine's warning dropped inside him. Lowe planned to lure him here to kill them both. Perhaps he thought he could eliminate everyone who could expose him to Isma'il's friend. He met

Sabine's eyes. She nodded once, a subtle reassurance. Even frightened, her eyes beamed her will. She trusted him.

He returned his attention to his aim. It hadn't moved. Sabine closed her eyes and dropped her weight. Lowe started to adjust his hold on her. Cullen fired three times in rapid succession.

Lowe's body crumpled to the floor, his head hitting a dirty white cabinet door, lolling until it went still, a stream of blood trailing from three holes in his forehead. The gun thudded to rest a few feet from his hand.

Sabine crawled backward until she came against Cullen's calves. Flipping the safety on his gun, he stuffed it in his boot and bent to slip his arms under hers, pulling her to her feet. She turned and threw her arms around him. He held her, burying his face in her hair, smelling her, feeling her tremble despite her bravery. He closed his eyes to the sensation of her alive in his arms. Safe. Once and for all.

"You're safe now," he said, swallowing because his heart was still pounding from the fear that had ripped through him.

He felt her relax against him. Her breathing slowed.

"I thought I lost you," he confessed, because it was so overwhelmingly true.

She leaned back, eyes red and face moist from tears. He watched his meaning take hold in her eyes. "You didn't."

"Yeah, but I thought I did, I was so…so…" Afraid. It appalled him to know what losing her could do to him. Shred his soul. Incapacitate him. Reduce him to a shaking mess of a man.

"You didn't lose me," she insisted.

He never wanted to feel like this again.

Chapter 13

Watching the landscape pass by the window of Cullen's rental car, Sabine's head pounded and it felt as if there was a heavy fog in her head. She had a slight concussion from being struck on the head by Lowe. But that was easy to ignore with Cullen's silence on the ride home from Denver.

They'd had to stay and talk to the police. They were probably only free to go because of Cullen's connections. It had still taken a few hours. She was tired...but mostly because of Cullen.

Did he think she hadn't noticed how his fear had driven him to withdraw? He had a glimpse of what it would feel like to lose her, so now he'd remove himself from the possibility of it ever happening again. Maybe he didn't want her to know how his fear had weakened him. Maybe it made him feel like less of a man to know he was capable of feeling so much for another person. Part of her took heart that he did, in fact, feel that much for her, but mostly she was disappointed. And mad.

She knew what was going to happen as soon as they arrived at her bookstore. He was going to leave.

Ironic, that she'd placed so much significance on his choosing her over his mission when that had never been the thing that would keep them apart. Watching his father ruin his life to alcoholism over a woman had made an irreversible imprint in his subconscious. It seemed they had that in common, although she was closer to resolving things with her father than he with his. The thought caught her unguarded. Was she ready to forgive her father? Maybe not quite, but in time she might. He wasn't the way she remembered, and in her heart she knew he was sincere in his desire to know her.

Cullen drove to a stop behind her bookstore, and her nerves turned her stomach. This was it. Time for goodbye. She resigned herself to letting Cullen go. It was all or nothing for her. She wanted all of him or nothing.

He left the car running and neither of them moved for a while. They'd escaped the media for now. Not even Minivan Man was here yet.

Finally, Sabine opened the car door and got out, hearing him do the same. At the foot of the stairs leading to her office door, she faced him. He came to a stop before her, and all she could do was look at his face. She couldn't imagine never seeing him again.

Those gray eyes found hers and they stared at each other. She felt his struggle, the difficulty he was having saying goodbye. So she put her hands on his chest and rose onto the balls of her feet. She pressed her lips to his. His hands went to her waist.

"Sabine…"

She stopped him by moving her hand to place a finger over his mouth. That mouth she loved kissing so much. "Don't," she said. Finding his eyes with hers, those gray eyes that were always so full of strength and vitality, she told him silently of her love.

"Do what you need to do, Cullen. Don't worry about me. I'm where I belong." She forced herself to smile, seeing his wary look. "If it weren't for you, I wouldn't be here right now. I wouldn't be looking forward to opening my bookstore and living a quiet life in a town I love. I'm safe and I have you to thank for that. I've got my bookstore and I'm going to be happy." Someday, she thought.

He closed his eyes and rested his forehead against hers. "I'm so sorry."

"I'm not," she whispered. And she wasn't. This wasn't the same as her parents. Sabine wouldn't let Cullen keep reappearing in her life if he chose to turn away from his feelings. She also would never regret believing they had a chance, because it was true. They had a chance. Cullen was just blowing it.

A moment passed. Two. Then he stepped back.

Sabine willed the sadness that numbed her to a manageable level. He was leaving. Turning his back on her, on what he felt for her, and what she felt for him. The risk to his heart was too great for him.

This was the way it had to be. He had to go and she had to let him. She didn't want a man whose heart wasn't totally hers. He had to be sure of his choices. And she couldn't help him decide.

"Goodbye, Cullen," she said, feeling tears brim her eyes. She turned so he wouldn't see them and climbed the stairs, opening her back door.

"Sabine…"

She closed the door and leaned her forehead against it. This was it. Cullen was out of her life.

She heard the rental car drive away.

Oh, God. It tore her from the inside out to hear him leave. Despite her best efforts, more tears filled her eyes and a few spilled free.

* * *

Cullen sat at his desk with his fingers in his hair, leaning over a pad of paper full of his scribbles. His attempt at starting over with a new business strategy.

The phone rang. At least the number still hadn't gotten out to the press, so he knew it wasn't a reporter.

"McQueen." There was no point in hiding his identity.

"You have very powerful friends."

The shock of surprise rendered him mute for a second. "Commander Birch."

"As much as I hate to admit it, I have to agree with Colonel Roth."

Hope singed his nerves. Roth had gone to see his commander?

"I'm not stupid, McQueen. I know there's more to that company of yours than the press is going on about. I knew you were good, but I never would have guessed you were that good."

"I'm sure you didn't call just to tell me that." If Birch was trying to pry information out of him, it wasn't going to work. He was still willing to sacrifice the army reserves to protect those who helped make a company like SCS possible.

"Colonel Roth explained to me how valuable you were to the Special Forces community. He also explained he wasn't going to allow a discharge. The only kind of action I can take…is no action at all."

Cullen leaned back in his chair, exultation and relief and gratitude so great it thrilled him for a few seconds.

"So you're still a part of this group," Birch continued. "Your reserve status remains what it was. However, I do recommend you work in intelligence from now on, rather than Ops. But as Colonel Roth put it in no uncertain terms, the choice is yours."

"Done. I'll move over to intelligence."

Birch's silence told him he'd gained back a little ground with his commander.

"For what it's worth, I'm sorry I had to go behind your back."

"I don't ever want to hear you mention this again, McQueen. If you have to run a private company, make sure it stays private from now on. Is that clear?"

"Yes, sir." In his head he roared another *yes!* And ended the call.

He hadn't lost his position with the army. And from the looks of it, he had backing for a new company.

Sabine's face pushed his elation down. Reporters still hung around the building, hoping to get him to talk about her. But his answer was always the same.

Sorry, no comment.

Did you go somewhere to be alone with her?

Sorry, no comment.

Why was someone trying to kill her? Are Aden Archer's and Casey Lowe's deaths related to her kidnapping?

Sorry, no comment.

Are you two still having an affair? Did she call things off or did you?

No comment, no comment.

Are you going to marry her?

That one always tripped him up.

All he had to do was recall how he'd felt after discovering Sabine missing, and it drove away any doubt he harbored over leaving her. He truly, absolutely, never wanted to feel like that again. He'd self-destruct.

It should be so clear to him. Get his company back on its feet. Move on. He could regroup. Start over. All he needed was a new plan.

"You look like hell."

Cullen slid his hand from his hair and looked up at Odie. She looked smart in her oval, black-rimmed glasses and dull gray suit with her long, thick black hair piled in a sexy mess on top of her head—deceptive cover for the strength that lay beneath the shell of a powerful woman.

"Thanks. Glad to see you, too."

She humphed and moved into the office. "When are you going to admit defeat and get on with your life?"

"Right now. I'm going to sell the building and start another company somewhere else. Hire a few more operatives."

"In Roaring Creek?" Her dark eyes slanted at him skeptically.

Odie wasn't stupid and he resented her audacity. "I don't know where."

With a roll of her hips, she planted her rear on his desk, right on top of the documents he'd been studying. "Look at yourself, Cullen." She used her forefinger to flick his uncombed hair. "When's the last time you showered?"

"This morning," he said, meeting her indomitable gaze.

"You didn't go home last night."

"Oh, yeah." He nodded, caught in the lie. "Yesterday morning then."

Every time he went home, he was suffocated by the emptiness that surrounded him. He couldn't believe he'd lived like that for so long. So alone and in such a sterile environment. He didn't even have any pictures of his family anywhere. Not that he wanted any of his dad.

"You're pathetic. You know that, don't you?"

"Just say what's on your mind, Odie." He leaned back in his chair and waited.

She didn't waste a beat. "It's painfully obvious you love her."

"No, I don't." He refused to believe it.

He didn't want to love a woman that much. It was precisely what he'd struggled to avoid all these years. That kind of love. The kind his father felt for his mother. The deepest kind. The kind a man could never walk away from. Even if death forced it upon him.

Odie's eyes narrowed in a shrewd study of him, then relaxed as she came to a conclusion. "You're running scared."

He felt his brow shoot low. "Now wait just a minute—"

"You're *afraid* to love her."

"I am not."

"You're scared to death, McQueen." She laughed with her re-alization. "That is so priceless. *You*. Afraid of a little ole thing like love."

Lifting her weight off the desk, she stood. "You know what? I'm going to do you a favor." She walked toward his office door with all the brass of a woman who could bring politicians to their knees.

What was she up to? When Odelia Frank started to use her brain, frightening things happened.

"What are you going to do?" It wasn't a question. He'd seen her like this before. When she took down the barriers standing in her way of ferreting out terrorists.

"First—" she turned in the doorway "—I'm going to put a For Sale sign up." She turned her back and headed for the front door. "Then I'm going to give you a little…*push*."

He looked out the window and inwardly kicked himself for not predicting this. A reporter sat in his car, a tan Malibu.

Cullen stood up from his chair so fast that it crashed to the floor. By the time he made it to the front door of SCS, Odie had a handwritten sign taped there and was sauntering toward the reporter.

Cullen shoved the door wider and approached. His steps slowed when he heard her talking.

"It's true he went somewhere to be alone with Sabine O'Clery," she was saying. "They stayed at Hotel Teatro in downtown Denver. Just the two of them…for days. They couldn't get enough of each other."

He hissed an expletive.

"Are they still having an affair?" The reporter wrote with a frenzy on his little note pad while the cameraman at his side filmed Odie's smug face.

"Oh, yeah. Things are steamier than ever between them. He just needs to tie up a few loose ends before he goes back to Roaring Creek."

"So, he's in love with her?"

Odie glanced at him with a wicked smile. "Why don't you ask *him* that."

The camera moved to Cullen and he froze on the sidewalk a few feet away.

The reporter and cameraman bustled closer to him.

"Are you in love with Sabine O'Clery, Mr. McQueen?" the reporter asked.

Envisioning millions of Americans watching this on the next newscast, the only face that really stood out was Sabine's. If he answered no, what would that say to her? If he answered yes, what would that mean for him?

The reporter smiled.

Cullen swallowed the dry lump in his throat.

Beside him, Odie smothered a giggle. She was enjoying the sight of his squirming on national television, that was for sure.

"Are you in love with the woman you rescued from Afghanistan, Mr. McQueen?"

All of the sudden it was so clear to him. Odie was right. He was scared and he'd run from something for the first time in his life. But running from Sabine wasn't going to save him the way his career had from the grief and anger he'd felt watching his father dwindle away and give up on everything. Cullen didn't want to run anymore. He wanted to take his greatest risk yet and go back to Sabine.

He looked right into the camera and said, "Yes."

* * *

"*Yes.*"

Sabine's knees stopped supporting her. She plopped down onto her mother's couch, staring at the television with a slack jaw. Cullen had just said the word.

Yes.

He loved her. He looked terrified, but he *loved her*.

A smile flickered and died with her disbelief.

"Are you going to marry her?" the reporter asked.

Sabine watched Cullen say, "Yes. If she'll have me." And her heart melted all over itself. He sounded so certain. She put her hand over her gaping mouth.

"Oh my Lord, *listen* to him," Mae said from behind her, incredulous. She sat down beside Sabine and together they watched Cullen pledge his love to Sabine O'Clery, the woman he'd rescued from Afghanistan.

"Did you fall in love when you were in Greece?"

Cullen looked dazed. "I didn't realize how much I love her until now."

"Now?"

"Yes. Now. Just a few minutes ago. Right now."

The reporter chuckled, clearly amused. "What about her? Does she feel the same about you?"

Cullen turned toward the camera. Sabine felt his unease. He didn't like the publicity but he was using the camera to communicate with her. The realization made her weak with love for him.

"That's exactly what I plan to find out," he said, turning.

Much later that day, Roaring Creek was teeming with media. Sabine paced inside her mother's cabin, biting her fingernails until there was nothing left.

She knew Cullen was in town, because a breaking news

update showed him entering the building across from her bookstore, a fact the media exploited with relish.

"You should go down there," Mae said from beside her. "This town will never be able to rest until you tell him you love him."

Sabine looked at her mother, nervous and excited at the same time.

"Go," her mother urged. "He's expecting you." Stepping closer, she handed Sabine the keys to the Jeep and gave her a push toward the door.

Knowing there was no arguing with her, Sabine left and drove into town. The throng of media sent her heart skipping anew. It looked different on television. Much more intimidating in person.

She parked behind her bookstore and wormed her way through the crowd of people asking questions, all with big smiles on their faces, loving the hype of her romance with the man who'd saved her life. It would take too long to explain it was more than that to her. She'd fallen in love with more than a hero.

Locking the door, she went to the front of her bookstore and opened the blinds. Cullen stood outside his building, squinting his eyes in the sunlight, made brighter by the reflection off the fresh layer of snow that had fallen. The sight of him sent a wave of anticipation through her.

He stepped off the sidewalk and strode across the street. His long, powerful legs moved with heavy grace in a pair of faded blue jeans. His arms swung at his sides, corded muscle beneath the soft material of his black henley. His black hair waved in a slight breeze. He looked good. All man walking toward her. An American hero. And he was all hers.

Reporters scurried like cockroaches from the back of her bookstore to the front. They swarmed around Cullen, shoving microphones in front of his face. His sure strides never faltered. He looked straight ahead, a man on a mission. She couldn't hear the reporters' questions, but the sound of their voices traveled through the window.

Unlocking the front door, she pulled it open and felt a rush seeing him standing, flesh and bone, in front of her. His eyes were intense and began to smolder. Clicks from the cameras went off behind him.

She stepped back as he entered. He closed the door without taking his gaze off her.

"How are you?" Cullen asked, love in his eyes and voice.

She smiled in answer. "Fine."

"Yeah?" he said.

"Yeah." Were they really having this ridiculous conversation while a horde of reporters waited outside to learn whether Sabine was going to marry him or not?

"I'm sorry I left you the way I did," he said.

A reporter shot their picture through the glass.

"Are you going to move in across the street?" she asked.

He nodded and shifted on his feet, rolling from his heels to his toes. "For now."

His nervousness was uncharacteristic but endearing. They were getting close to The Question. "What are you going to do? I mean, for a living?"

"I thought I'd open a mountaineering shop."

"Across the street?"

"Yeah."

She wasn't fooled. "That would give you good cover." He could never remove himself from Special Ops completely. It was in his blood. "I mean, when all the publicity dies down."

He glanced back at the window to another camera-clicking flurry. When he faced forward, a slight grin creased the side of his mouth. "You think it'll die down?"

She laughed softly and he stepped closer. With one arm, he hooked her waist and pulled her against him. She didn't have to look to know the cameras were going wild on the other side of the window. She put her hands on his chest.

"Might as well make it worth their while," he said.

"Yeah?"

"Yeah." His husky voice made her heart pound faster.

He closed the space between their lips. She couldn't hear the camera pings but knew they were going off outside the window. Her ears were humming too much from the impassioned rate of her heartbeat.

He lifted his head and looked down at her.

"Let's go upstairs," she said.

"Does that mean you're going to marry me?"

"I'll marry you a thousand times."

He grinned wider than before. "Really? A thousand?"

"Ten thousand."

"In that case, wait here."

Stepping back, he turned to the door. Swinging it open, the click and ping of cameras went off again.

"She said yes!" he shouted, and the crowd cheered.

* * * * *

The Colton family is back!
Enjoy a sneak preview of
COLTON'S SECRET SERVICE
by Marie Ferrarella, part of
THE COLTONS: FAMILY FIRST *miniseries.*
Available from Silhouette Romantic Suspense
in September 2008.

He cautioned himself to be leery. He was human and he'd been conned before. But never by anyone nearly so attractive. Never by anyone he'd felt so attracted to.

In her defense, Nick supposed that Georgie could actually be telling him the truth. That she was a victim in all this. He had his people back in California checking her out, to make sure she was who she said she was and had, as she claimed, not even been near a computer but on the road these last few months that the threats had been made.

In the meantime, he was doing his own checking out. Up close and exceedingly personal. So personal he could feel his blood stirring.

It had been a long time since he'd thought of himself as anything other than a law enforcement agent of one type or other. But Georgeann Grady made him remember that beneath the oaths he had taken and his devotion to duty, there beat the heart of a man.

A man who'd been far too long without the touch of a woman.

He watched as the light from the fireplace caressed the outline of Georgie's small, trim, jean-clad body as she moved about the rustic living room that could have easily come off the set of a Hollywood Western. Except that it was genuine.

As genuine as she claimed to be?

Something inside of him hoped so.

He wasn't supposed to be taking sides. His only interest in being here was to guarantee Senator Joe Colton's safety as the latter continued to make his bid for the presidency. Everything else was supposed to be secondary, but, Nick had to silently admit, that was just a wee bit hard to remember right now.

Earlier, before she'd put her precocious handful of a daughter to bed, Georgie had fed his appetite by whipping up some kind of a delicious concoction out of the vegetables she'd pulled from her garden. Vegetables that, by all rights, should have been withered and dried. She'd mentioned that a friend came by on occasion to weed and tend it. Still, it surprised him that somehow she'd managed to make something mouthwatering out of it.

Almost as mouthwatering as she looked to him right at this moment.

Again, he was reminded of the appetite that hadn't been fed, hadn't been satisfied.

And wasn't going to be, Nick sternly told himself. At least not now. Maybe later, when things took on a more definite shape and all the questions in his head were answered to his satisfaction, there would be time to explore this feeling. This woman. But not now.

Damn it.

"Sorry about the lack of light," Georgie said, breaking into his train of thought as she turned around to face him. If she noticed the way he was looking at her, she gave no indication. "But I don't see a point in paying for electricity if I'm not going to be here. Besides, Emmie really enjoys camping out. She likes roughing it."

"And you?" Nick asked, moving closer to her, so close that a whisper would have trouble fitting in. "What do you like?"

The very breath stopped in Georgie's throat as she looked up at him.

"I think you've got a fair shot of guessing that one," she told him softly.

* * * * *

Be sure to look for COLTON'S SECRET SERVICE
and the other following titles from
THE COLTONS: FAMILY FIRST *miniseries:*
RANCHER'S REDEMPTION by Beth Cornelison
THE SHERIFF'S AMNESIAC BRIDE by Linda Conrad
SOLDIER'S SECRET CHILD by Caridad Piñeiro
BABY'S WATCH by Justine Davis
A HERO OF HER OWN by Carla Cassidy

Silhouette®

Romantic
SUSPENSE

**Sparked by Danger,
Fueled by Passion.**

The Coltons Are Back!

Marie Ferrarella
Colton's Secret Service

The Coltons: Family First

On a mission to protect a senator, Secret Service agent
Nick Sheffield tracks down a threatening message only
to discover Georgie Gradie Colton, a rodeo-riding single
mom, who insists on her innocence. Nick is instantly
taken with the feisty redhead, but vows not to let his
feelings interfere with his mission. Now he must figure
out if this woman is conning him or if he can trust her
and the passion they share....

Available September wherever books are sold.

Visit Silhouette Books at www.eHarlequin.com   SRS27598

Silhouette *Desire*

Billionaires and Babies

MAUREEN CHILD
BABY BONANZA

Newly single mom Jenna Baker has only one thing on her mind: child support for her twin boys. Ship owner and carefree billionaire Nick Falco discovers he's a daddy—brought on by a night of passion a year ago. Nick may be ready to become a father, but is he ready to become a groom when he discovers the passion that still exists between him and Jenna?

Available September
wherever books are sold.

Always Powerful, Passionate and Provocative.

REQUEST YOUR FREE BOOKS!

2 FREE NOVELS PLUS 2 FREE GIFTS!

Silhouette® Romantic

SUSPENSE

Sparked by Danger, Fueled by Passion!

YES! Please send me 2 FREE Silhouette® Romantic Suspense novels and my 2 FREE gifts (gifts are worth about $10). After receiving them, if I don't wish to receive any more books, I can return the shipping statement marked "cancel." If I don't cancel, I will receive 4 brand-new novels every month and be billed just $4.24 per book in the U.S. or $4.99 per book in Canada, plus 25¢ shipping and handling per book plus applicable taxes, if any*. That's a savings of at least 15% off the cover price! I understand that accepting the 2 free books and gifts places me under no obligation to buy anything. I can always return a shipment and cancel at any time. Even if I never buy another book from Silhouette, the two free books and gifts are mine to keep forever.

240 SDN EEX6 340 SDN EEYJ

Name _____ (PLEASE PRINT)

Address _____ Apt. #

City _____ State/Prov. _____ Zip/Postal Code

Signature (if under 18, a parent or guardian must sign)

Mail to the **Silhouette Reader Service:**
IN U.S.A.: P.O. Box 1867, Buffalo, NY 14240-1867
IN CANADA: P.O. Box 609, Fort Erie, Ontario L2A 5X3

Not valid to current subscribers of Silhouette Romantic Suspense books.

Want to try two free books from another line?
Call 1-800-873-8635 or visit www.morefreebooks.com.

* Terms and prices subject to change without notice. N.Y. residents add applicable sales tax. Canadian residents will be charged applicable provincial taxes and GST. Offer not valid in Quebec. This offer is limited to one order per household. All orders subject to approval. Credit or debit balances in a customer's account(s) may be offset by any other outstanding balance owed by or to the customer. Please allow 4 to 6 weeks for delivery. Offer available while quantities last.

Your Privacy: Silhouette is committed to protecting your privacy. Our Privacy Policy is available online at www.eHarlequin.com or upon request from the Reader Service. From time to time we make our lists of customers available to reputable third parties who may have a product or service of interest to you. If you would prefer we not share your name and address, please check here. ☐

SRS08R

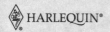

Inside ROMANCE

Stay up-to-date on all your romance reading news!

The Inside Romance newsletter is a FREE quarterly newsletter highlighting our upcoming series releases and promotions!

Click on the <u>Inside Romance</u> link on the front page of **www.eHarlequin.com** or e-mail us at insideromance@harlequin.ca to sign up to receive your FREE newsletter today!

You can also subscribe by writing us at: HARLEQUIN BOOKS Attention: Customer Service Department P.O. Box 9057, Buffalo, NY 14269-9057

Please allow 4-6 weeks for delivery of the first issue by mail.

IHINBPA10R

Silhouette®

Romantic

SUSPENSE

COMING NEXT MONTH

#1527 NATURAL-BORN PROTECTOR—Carla Cassidy
Wild West Bodyguards
When Melody Thompson returns to her hometown to investigate her
sister's murder, she runs straight into a mysterious and intriguing neighbor,
ex-rancher-turned-bodyguard Hank Tyler. The killer comes for Melody,
and only Hank can keep her safe—but will their instant attraction put them
in even greater danger?

#1528 COLTON'S SECRET SERVICE—Marie Ferrarella
The Coltons: Family First
On a mission to protect a senator, Secret Service agent Nick Sheffield
tracks down a threatening message, only to discover Georgie Gradie
Colton. The rodeo-riding single mom insists on her innocence. Nick is
taken with the feisty redhead, and he must figure out if this woman is
conning him or if he can trust her and the passion they share....

#1529 INTIMATE ENEMY—Marilyn Pappano
A secret admirer turned stalker sends lawyer Jamie Munroe into hiding in
the least likely of places—the home of ex-lover Russ Calloway. Russ and
Jamie have a stormy history, but his code of honor won't let him stand idly
by while her life is in danger. Being so close again brings up emotions that
may be just as risky....

#1530 MERCENARY'S HONOR—Sharron McClellan
Running for her life in Colombia, reporter Fiona Macmillan needs
mercenary Angel Castillo's help. She has an incriminating tape of the
Colombian head of national security executing a woman, and the man will
kill to get it back. Now Fiona and Angel must learn to trust each other—
and resist giving in to passion—to escape with their lives.

SRSCNM0808